# My life is a girdle

Random House Australia Pty Ltd
20 Alfred Street, Milsons Point NSW 2061
http://www.randomhouse.com.au

Sydney New York Toronto
London Auckland Johannesburg
and agencies throughout the world

First published in 2003
Text and illustrations copyright © Gretel Killeen 2003

National Library of Australia
Cataloguing-in-Publication Data

Killeen, Gretel.
   My life is a girdle.

   For teenage readers.
   ISBN 1 74051 899 3.

   I. Title.

A823.3

Cover photograph designed by Gretel Killeen.
Cover photograph by Jenny Hearder.
Photograph of the author by Derek Henderson.
Typeset by Asset Typesetting Pty Ltd in 12/16 Palladia.
Printed by Griffin Press Pty Ltd, Adelaide.

10 9 8 7 6 5 4 3 2 1

# My life is a girdle

# GRETEL KILLEEN

RANDOM HOUSE AUSTRALIA

*This book is dedicated to my family,*
*without whom I wouldn't be here*
*(because I wouldn't have been born).*

# February 3rd
*In the hallway of our house approximately one month before MY BIRTHDAY*

**7 am**

Dear Brand New Diary,
    Bonjour et cetera. Let me introduce myself.
    My name is Fleur Trotter and I am the tortured daughter of my two parents who are divorced and yet still live in the same house along with their new husband and wife (who are called the Pip and Babette). I also live with my two sisters and a grandma who doesn't so much live with us as sort of 'life support with us' instead. My kind-of-boyfriend Dwayne did live with us but now he doesn't. (Please Note: He's not dead or anything.)
    My so-called 'family' and I live a billion miles away from anything useful in a house that can probably best be described as indescribable. So imagine whatever you want but try to include olive green shaggy carpet with a kind of vomit pattern on it, striped beige wallpaper with a sort of squashed dead insect pattern on it, stiff itchy grass in the garden and a pet fish finger in the fridge.

As you know, you are my third diary. Oh no you're not, I just remembered, you're my fourth, but anyway even if you did know that, what you probably don't know is that you are also maybe-possibly-perhaps my last diary. You see my birthday is coming up which means that soon I will be officially a year older and I will then be the age when you should stop writing in your diary, dye your hair blonde, do one million sit-ups every day, date Justin Timberlake and start churning out mega-hit pop songs. My first song is going to be called *My Sisters are Miss Priss and Bum Face*, and the chorus to it will be lots of people making farting sounds. My second single is going to be called *My Stepmother is a Frog, My Stepfather is a Toad*. And my third song is going to be called *My Grandma is a Nymphomaniac Even Though She Looks Like a Bleached Prune Wearing a Grey Wool Wig*.

I have absolutely no musical talent but I don't think that will be a problem. I mean, I've got more than the Spice Girls ever had and just look how far they got. Well they got quite far for a very brief period of time and then they disbanded, married, divorced and developed eating disorders (but I understand in the music industry this is considered to be a successful career).

Actually I shouldn't joke about other people's misfortunes. And I probably shouldn't joke about my grandmother looking like a prune in a wig, because she went orange yesterday. Going orange in our family is a sure sign that you've either been standing very close to the microwave for way too long, you've eaten too many carrots, or you are perhaps about to die. In most families people go white when they're about to die because their heart and lungs can't pump the blood and oxygen through their body effectively but in our family we go orange, presumably because God wants us to be like traffic lights and warn those around us that somebody's big red stop sign is about to go on.

My grandma has turned orange several times in her life but so far it's been because she purposefully and liberally covered herself in cheap fake tan (otherwise known as shoe polish). She does this sort of thing to get more attention because my grandmother has an adult version of Attention Deficit Disorder. This means she panics if people aren't paying her enough attention.

Personally I think making yourself change colour in order to get people's sympathy is so absolutely manipulative and brilliant that it makes me quite jealous — so the last four

3

times Grandma's made herself go orange for attention, I've punished her by putting a sign outside her room that says 'DO NOT ENTER. HIGHLY CONTAGIOUS. COMPLETE ISOLATION REQUIRED.'

To be honest, I don't know where my grandmother gets this dramatic side from. It certainly isn't from my parents because the most dramatic thing my parents have ever done is serve red cordial with Wednesday night's rissoles and then call the meal *A Taste of Italy*.

My grandmother has done lots of other things in the past to get attention. She's sent love letters to Prince Harry, and she's posed nude for that magazine called *Pensioners Monthly*, so it's never really been a surprise when she's gone orange. The difficult thing is to decide whether or not she really is ill. I mean, you don't want to be in a situation where you're out sitting in the living room staring at your siblings wondering where they fit into the evolutionary chain and meanwhile your grandma drops dead in her bedroom. And then you don't find her for perhaps two days and when you do she's sort of holding up a sign that says 'I told you so'.

I told you so

But I guess the problem is that I'm not really thinking clearly at all at the moment because it's been a rough few days. Firstly of course there's the fact that my grandma may or may not be about to die which is a terrible shock because even though she's manipulative, childish, and self-obsessed, she is the person I relate to best in this house because she's the most like me.

I mean, what I mean is, that my grandma is the person I relate to best now that Dwayne doesn't live here anymore. He was my love, my life, my rock, my slave, but now he's gone and this has been the second shock. To tell you the truth, I can't really tell you the truth about how I feel about this loss. I've tried to listen to the radio to discover poetic lyrics that might define the complexities of my emotions but so far I've only found songs with titles like *You're So Sexy*

*Baby* and *I Want To Do It With You,* and to be honest, they just don't suit Dwayne. I mean, I'm sure someone would find him sexy and want to 'do it' with him, someone somewhere on a desert island who was blind and obviously desperate ... like my grandma, for example. But I never felt like this about Dwayne I just ... I just ... Oh doesn't matter.

Anyway, enough of this talk about Dwayne and Grandma because the actual worst thing that's happened is I've grown a zit the size of Mt Everest on my forehead. So that's three bad bits of news:

1/ my grandma appears to be dying;

2/ Dwayne has dumped me and moved out, and

3/ I have a big zit on my forehead (but I would like to point out right here and now that the first and second bits of bad news were not caused by the third bit).

When the world's most enormous pimple first erupted on my forehead I was completely ashamed and humiliated. And not surprisingly, now that it's been there for three whole days and shows absolutely no sign at all of ever leaving my face, I still feel ashamed and humiliated. This has not been helped by the fact that the first morning the zit appeared I went into the kitchen with it glaring on my forehead and my mother asked me if I'd like an extra bowl of cereal for my new friend.

It has of course occurred to me that this pimple might be the result of the stress I've experienced through Grandma or perhaps Dwayne. It has also occurred to me that this pimple might actually be the spirit of Dwayne, still haunting me in his physical absence, angry and red, weeping pussy tears that say 'You need to take a long hard look at yourself, Fleur!' But then again, it has also occurred to me that this zit might just be a zit.

Anyway, hopefully it's not permanent. The only person I know who has a permanent pimple is my stepfather, the Pip, and he's got it on his bum. AND IT'S ENORMOUS! Normally I wouldn't know this sort of thing about someone but you do feel sort of compelled to ask when you notice that every single time that person sits down, one half of their bum is still hovering five centimetres off the seat, because that person is SITTING ON HIS MASSIVE BUTT ZIT.

So I am a little bit worried that the zit on my forehead may never go away but if it doesn't and worst comes to worst and I can't become a ginormous intergalactic pop star because my forehead won't fit through the stage door, then I guess I'll just follow my Plan

B for life, which is to join a circus as Wanda the Two-headed Woman.

My mother says that you shouldn't worry about having a pimple on your head because your real friends will still like you. In fact, my mother says that the first time she went on a date with my dad she went so far as to actually make a pimple out of plasticine and custard and stick it on her forehead so that she could test whether my father truly loved her for who she was. My mother said he passed the test by telling her she looked beautiful that night ... but I reckon this conversation might have just proved that he actually really loves pimples.

Anyway, apparently if I keep applying our famous family recipe for pimple eradication I should have a blemish-free forehead within two more days. Mind you, my older sister, Miss Priss, applied the treatment to the volcano on her shoulder once and her whole body turned into a pimple. (Well, that's her excuse anyway.)

I'll write again in a second,

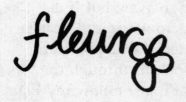

Dear Diary, Hellooooo again!

Where was I? Oh yes. So anyway, I'm going to be very busy in the time running up to my birthday because within the next month I have to get rid of my pimple, save my grandma's life and see if I want to rescue my relationship with Dwayne ... and while I'm doing all that, dear Dairy, I have to stay dedicated to you and write down all the complex and wondrous experiences of my life ... or at least steal them from other people and pretend that they're mine.

Anyway, enough about me. Let's talk instead about how worried I am about the situations with Grandma and Dwayne. Oh yes, I find both of these situations absolutely devastating because if I lose both Grandma and Dwayne just before my birthday then ......

# I'll end up with two less presents!

Of course as you know, present giving is not a big art in my family. This isn't surprising really, because my family has very little money and a negative quantity of style. You see, my family is obsessed with 'cheap and low maintenance' rather than 'attractive and useful'. (You may recall that I said our family pet was a frozen fish finger, well most of my parents' friends are blow-up dolls.) For a thousand years my mother has given me a can of beetroot for Christmas and for the first years of my life the greatest joy I knew was watching all the other kids in our street play with their new toys while I played with the boxes they came in.

The best present my family ever gave me, in terms of actual possible joy-potential was an inflatable tree. You could take it anywhere, blow it up and then just lie under its shade. As you can probably guess, the tree was sort of a really great idea but the only problem was that every time I lay under it, stray dogs would come and wee on me.

Still, any present is better than no present at all. Well no, actually now that I think about it that's not completely true. I mean, in retrospect I probably could have lived without the artificial leg my sister Bum Face gave me when I was nine and the rash Babette accidentally gave me last Christmas. One year my neighbour gave me a rubber band, but my parents wouldn't let me keep it because they said it was too dangerous.

My family really has this thing about danger in the house. A few years ago my stepfather, the Pip, fell asleep while drinking a glass of water and nearly drowned, so none of us has been allowed to drink a glass of water since. In fact, there were some discussions about whether or not we should be allowed to have a shower or even clean our teeth. (And the weird thing is that the Pip only fell asleep in the first place because he was talking at the same time while he was drinking the water and his own conversation made him nod off with boredom ... so I reckon we should be allowed to drink water and just forbid the Pip from speaking.)

Oh, and another thing we're not allowed to do is eat celery, because my stepmother, Babette, accidentally poked herself in the eye with a stick of celery and as a consequence nearly went blind. Personally I think it's a bit of a pity she didn't go blind in one eye, or even both, because then she might dress a little better.

Babette is currently wearing a very exciting pantsuit ensemble she made for herself out of egg cartons. She's sitting rather uncomfortably next to her husband, my father, on the couch that my mother knitted. Dad is wearing an ensemble that matches Babette's, and they look almost identical except that Dad's bosoms fill the egg cups a bit more adequately than

Babette's. Sitting next to my dad is my older sister, Miss Priss, who is wearing her usual cloud of gloom, and next to her is Bum Face whose outfit you never really notice because your eyes are so distracted by the fact that her face looks exactly like a bum. Sitting opposite Bum Face is my mother, wearing the delightful kaftan that she knitted using the leftover wool from the couch. Draped like a slug next to my mum is the Pip, wearing his latest beige tracksuit with what looks like not a pair of socks but an entire load of washing stuffed into the crotch area.

All my relatives are seated in a sort of circle in the living room and my grandmother is in the middle of them all lying on the floor. (She was going to be seated in the corner on the armchair my mother made out of papier-mache in the shape of a banana, but unfortunately as soon as my grandma sat down it became painfully obvious that the yellow of the banana clashed with the orange of her skin and so now Grandma's lying on the olive green vomit print carpet because it's a better complement to her complexion.)

'So, what are they doing?' I hear you ask, dear Dairy. Well, they're all having a 'family meeting', and even though I was invited I decided not to attend:

1/ because I've spent my whole life denying these people actually are my family and I don't feel like undoing all that hard work right now and

2/ because I'm hoping that the meeting might be about the surprise birthday party they're organising for me, in which case I think it might inhibit their creative flow and brain storming if I'm actually there. (Mind you, in retrospect I wish I had attended last year's family meeting for my surprise birthday party because the big surprise was that they decided not to give me a party.)

Yes, sub-human.

**7.03 and a half am**

Dear Diary,

Oh suddenly I feel soooooooooooooooooooooo alone. I miss Dwayne. It's sad really, to stand here and look at my family and be confronted by the fact that Dwayne is no longer with us.

For the last year Dwayne would have been present at a family meeting like this, but now he isn't here and I don't know where he is. On the day we broke up he just emptied his room, packed his bag, looked through the newspaper, made a phone call and walked through a wall.

**Actually on second thoughts ...**

He didn't actually walk through a wall. Well he did, but only because there was a door in the wall that he opened and then walked through. (Strange how the story can change so dramatically when all you add is a little bit of detail.)

Anyway, it was really weird how we separated. It sort of started all of a sudden. One minute we were sitting together on the roof looking at the view while I picked the occasional blackhead on Dwayne's back, and the next thing you know, he slid off the roof.

And that's when it started, or actually that's when it began to finish, because Dwayne hurt his ankle and had to go to casualty and the nurse who put the bandage on Dwayne's ankle seemed to think he was cute. But I didn't care, so despite what Dwayne said later, I wasn't jealous of the nurse's bosoms or her hair or her pert little butt and I only said, 'My God, that is the most pathetic bandage job I have ever seen anyone apply' because I was concerned about Dwayne's well-being. I mean, I think I know what I was talking about, I've done a two-day first aid course so let's get this straight, if the course had lasted about four years and three hundred and sixty-two days longer I could have been a doctor!

I've taken a pulse, I've done the Heimlich manoeuvre! I've tied a bandage around someone's head, and that's a lot more delicate than a stupid ankle. And even though that person's whole head and face did start to go red and then a bit purple and then the person passed out, I have nevertheless had a person's head in my hands and tied a piece of gauze around it (which many would call a bandage and some would call a tourniquet).

So anyway, so there!

When I was in Year Seven I gave mouth-to-mouth to a boy in Year Ten even when he didn't want or require it!

And that just goes to show how thorough and conscientious I am (or how cute he must have been).

So anyway back to Dwayne's ankle, because I just don't think Dwayne can go telling me that I only said the bandage was wrong because I was consumed with petty jealousy! And actually even though now I think about it I know that Dwayne didn't actually go telling me that, I think I know that that's what he was thinking. I mean, that's what I would have been thinking if the roles were reversed. In fact, that's what I was thinking even when the roles weren't reversed. Oh yes, even when I was telling Nurse Bosoms that the bandage was 'a joke', I was definitely thinking to myself, 'Fleur, don't say critical things just out of petty jealousy', and that's why I know that I didn't just say it out of petty jealousy ... because I told myself specifically not to! And if there's one thing I can be guaranteed to do it's completely concentrate on everything I'm talking about.

Now where was I and what was I talking about?

Ah yes, my relationship. The break-up. The ... oh I remember now, falling off the roof and the nurse and the bandage and my helpful advice. And yes, that's right, and why Dwayne doesn't live here anymore, because bizarrely somehow or other, some way or what not, the whole relationship weirdly and unexpectedly started to unravel after the Nurse Pert Butt Big Bosoms incident.

Please Note: I should point out that it did

NOT come to a crashing halt BECAUSE of the Nurse Pert Butt incident. Oh no, it came to a crashing halt after a rumour was spread about some guy called Balderzak De-navel sharing a tiny-weeny kiss with some very attractive, intelligent, vivacious and desirable girl whose name just happened to be Fleur Trotter!

And who could have spread such a salacious rumour? I hear you ask.

Well . . . . . . . . . . . . . . . . . . . . . . . . me, of course.

So anyway, it was after that that Dwayne dumped me. Well actually, he didn't dump me, he asked me if the rumour was true. And I remember thinking that the facts aren't true but he had heard the rumour right, so I said yes. And then he made a face like a goldfish dying of thirst and walked through the wall.

It's all come as bit of a shock. Not so much the rumour about me , because I was prepared for that (because I spread it), but the fact that Dwayne has left my life. I'd call him but I don't know where he is, so I'm feeling a bit lost. I would imagine this is a bit like how you'd feel if one of your arms just suddenly fell off. You know, a bit off balance, a bit vulnerable, a bit incapable of using a can-opener effectively.

I mean, I know that time heels all wounds and even though my arm can't actually grow back I will learn to use a can-opener again, but that doesn't make this suffering any easier. I mean, I know what people say about love and loss. I know there are plenty more fish in the sea and that people in glass houses shouldn't walk around in the nude, but at the moment all these profundities mean nothing to me because I only have one arm.

I try to see the upside of this situation but I can't, because there appear to me to be only two downsides. I guess if I really tried hard I could maybe ...

Nup, I can't.
There are only two downsides.

Oh no, wait a minute, I can see a bit of an upside way over there in the distance!

Oh no never mind, it wasn't an upside after all, it was just the cat's bum.

### 7.05 and a tiny little bit am

Dear Diary,

I suppose at least now I can relate to other people's pain and suffering a bit better.
At least now, for example, I feel a little bit closer to understanding the loss that the Pip must have felt when he was a teenager and his parents threw away the family wheelbarrow because the school psychologist said that the Pip had developed an unnatural attraction to it.

No actually, on second thoughts, I still don't understand that at all.

But anyway, maybe I'm better off without Dwayne here. I mean, Dwayne was so loving and so supportive and maybe I just need a bit more of a challenge. Maybe I should see what it would be like to have a boyfriend like my best friend Lurline's boyfriend, who never rings her when he says he's going to, always turns up really late, and ignores her when they go to parties. Yeah, maybe I need that, because when someone treats you that badly all the time, the weird thing is that you feel quite special when they finally do give you a crumb of attention. It's like being on an eternal diet and occasionally breaking out for a piece of chocolate cake.

(Please Note: Not a piece of chocolate cake that my mother cooked, of course, because that would sit in your stomach like a brick for a week, then make you fart for a month and finally give you chronic diarrhoea for about a year.)

Another Note: You know I just realised that with most food that you shouldn't eat, people always quote that saying 'A moment on the lips, a lifetime on the hips', but with my mother's cooking it's a moment on the lips and a lifetime on the toilet.

A Toilet
(not a hat)

Anyway, back to Lurline being eternally rejected by her boyfriend. Well, the other good thing about her situation is that even though she doesn't get a lot of attention from her boyfriend as a result of her relationship, it actually means she gets heaps and heaps from us, because she's always bursting into tears and needing a hug, and having to miss out on sport because her big bug-red eyes are so sore from crying that it would be dangerous for her to try and catch a ball. And it's not only us who give her a hug, it's complete strangers and cute guys in Year Twelve. I mean, it's so dramatic and so fabulously touchy-touchy, and judging by Lurline's experience it's also an excellent way to have a grope with some hunky-spunky guy while pretending you're just too distraught to realise that while you're hugging him your hands have slipped from his shoulders and are now clutching his bum cheeks.

Oh Lurline's relationship is so Shakespearian, and I absolutely love that. Her relationship is like *Days of Our Lives*. Dwayne and my relationship was like a gardening program on the ABC. Honestly, if anyone asked me 'How are you and Dwayne going?' I always said great. It was so predictable, so unsurprising, so much like we'd been married for forty-two years. It was like that movie *The Truman Show,* with a labrador called Goldie who always greeted our guests by trying to mate with their legs.

It was so nice it was dull. And that's why I started those rumours about Balderzak's tongue tickling my tonsils (i.e. kissing). I regret them now because they outraged everyone and I only started the rumours because I wanted to add a little bit of spice to my relationship with Dwayne. I wanted him to get jealous, I didn't want him to leave me. I wanted him to have to fight for me, I wanted to ... I wanted to be like J-Lo and Ben Affleck, or Melanie Griffith, or Gwyneth Paltrow, or someone who's actually relevant to this metaphor. Of course I never kissed Balderzak De-navel. I mean, he's so good looking and so well dressed he is more than likely definitely gay.

When we broke up Dwayne was really, really upset and said that I should take 'a good long look at myself' but I couldn't because we don't have any mirrors in our house. No, they all cracked the day my stepmother, Babette, moved in. Dad replaced them cheaply using aluminium foil but they don't work as mirrors and if you stand near one in summer you can feel yourself begin to bake.

So anyway, there you go. Dwayne has gone, and after more than a year together it's pretty weird getting used to life without him. I mean, I know I should feel free and ready to run wild through these streets of Moronville wearing nothing but ug boots on my head, but instead I feel like one of those elephants in India or Africa or somewhere — you know, where they chain the baby elephant to a stick for a few years and then they take the chain away but the elephant still stays near the stick for the rest of its life. Yes, I am metaphorically the elephant and the relationship I had with Dwayne is the metaphorical stick (or perhaps the metaphorical chain, or perhaps the metaphorical elephant pooh).

I think my response to Dwayne's absence is completely understandable. Dwayne had been living with us since his parents spontaneously combusted in a bizarre gumboot accident a year ago. This occurred shortly after my parents drove into his parents' car and shortly after we lived in their caravan park during a drought and a flood and then all escaped on a massive boat that Dwayne built using nails, old floorboards and soggy fruitcakes as glue. For some strange reason my parents always felt themselves to be responsible for the spontaneous combustion incident and so asked newly orphaned Dwayne if he'd like to come and live in our weird little world with stepmums and stepdads and divorced parents and sicko sisters and a nympho granny all in the one house. And poor desperate Dwayne said yes.

I guess it's been a big responsibility for all of us, taking in a young virile boy who is obviously irresistibly attracted to me. I've had to look as un-beautiful as I can in case I accidentally turned Dwayne on and he's had to look as unattractive as he can so he doesn't turn Grandma on. And then of course there's been the added problem of his genetic propensity for spontaneous combustion, which has meant that for the entire year we've had to take it in turns to make sure that, no matter where Dwayne goes, one member of the family is always standing next to him with a hose.

Oh dear,

**7.06 am**
*Still in the hallway*

Dear Diary,
   Anyway back to me again. At the moment I am still standing in the hall outside the living room, which by the way is a room that is so unattractive and so claustrophobic that its name should be changed to the 'slowly dying' room. I wanted to eavesdrop on the family's meeting in the traditional way by pressing one end of a glass against the door and the other against my ear but unfortunately, because of my mother's NO DANGEROUS, SHARP OR ATTRACTIVE OBJECTS IN THE HOUSE policy we don't actually have any glass glasses

in the house so I'm eavesdropping with a styrofoam party cup.

Please Note: I probably shouldn't tell you this but even the Pip's reading glasses have been replaced by two plastic bottle tops.

Please Note: The reason why I probably shouldn't tell you that is not because it's rude to talk about someone behind their back but because the Pip doesn't realise that his reading glasses are made out of plastic and I don't want him to ever read this and find out.

But then again, I've just realised there's no chance in the world that he'll be successfully reading this because, considering his reading glasses are made of plastic bottle tops, the only things he will ever be able to read with his so-called glasses on are the messages inside the bottle tops — you know, things like *Congratulations you've won a new car*, or *Hey you're a winner*.

But then again he's never going to read these messages because I made the Pip's 'glasses' and I know for a fact that the messages inside the Pip's lids say *You are not a winner* and *Bad luck, loser*. Hey, maybe that's why he walks around looking so depressed.

Interesting,

**7.07 am**

Dear Diary,

I just interrupted the meeting by calling out to Mum and asking her if we had anything other than styrofoam cups in the house and she said I could try drinking from a thermos or the saucepan. She then said that I should hurry up and come on and join the meeting because they're 'discussing something very important'.

Yeah sure. The last time I fell for that one I joined the meeting only to learn that the family was thinking of banning feet in the house because Bum Face had just tripped over someone's slipper and this means that feet are obviously dangerous.

Ooby dooby,

**7.09 am**

Dear Diary,

Okay, well after searching the entire house the only glass objects of any kind that I've managed to find have been my grandmother's teeth, which I actually suspect are made of plasticine not glass. But I also found a glass-shaped Tupperware container which has one of Bum Face's cockroaches in it ... the cockroach that she calls 'Boyfriend'.

I know this isn't how you're supposed to eavesdrop but it's all I've got. So now I'm eavesdropping using the Tupperware container with the cockroach in it and I swear if that cockroach manages to excavate its way through the lid and then burrows into my ear and then scratches its way through to my brain until I go completely insane then I am going to sue Bum Face for all she's worth (a beanie made out of an old toilet seat cover, a brooch that used to be a paper clip, and a facial expression that could be used by enemy powers as the ultimate weapon of mass destruction).

Blah,

## 7.09 and a half am

Dear Diary,

  I actually can't hear anything through the cockroach container, but I would imagine my family is having exactly the same argument they have every year about what day my birthday actually is. Mum will say it's next week and the stupid Pip will say he's absolutely positive it's not for two more years. My father will say my birthday is definitely not until October because he's sure I was conceived the night he and Mum went to the annual Porn and Prawn Bingo Night at the local RSL. In reply to this Mum will say she doesn't know what he's talking about so Dad will go on to say that he's surprised and hurt that she doesn't remember that particular slap-up romantic evening. And then Mum will say she's surprised she doesn't remember any slap-up romantic evening too, because if it did happen then it's the only one they ever had ... if you exclude the time Dad got drunk while taking Communion at his boss's wedding and decided to perform the full monty during the Lord's Prayer.

  Anyway, then Babette will say that she thinks I was born on the sixth hour of the sixth day of the sixth month because 666 is the devil's number. And my grandma will nod in agreement, despite the fact that she is more of a devil than me. I mean, at least I don't report myself as missing and then go hide in the neighbour's shrubbery, like my grandmother does. And even if I did report myself missing and go and hide in the neighbour's shrubbery I'm absolutely positive that I wouldn't make sure I was nude when the policemen came to find me! Which is what my grandmother does!

### 7.11 am

Wait a minute, dear Diary, I'm going to have to stop writing for a sec because I think my family knows that I'm eavesdropping. I guess someone or other has spotted my reflection in the portrait of Grandpa that was painted on the same day that his head was accidentally sucked up a rhino's bum and had to be pulled out with a vacuum cleaner. (Needless to say, Grandpa's expression is not the best and his hairdo is absolutely appalling.) Anyway, the point is that my family has started whispering to presumably stop me from hearing a word of what they're saying and now I can't hear a word that they're saying.

This is actually very annoying because I need to go to the toilet and I was kind of hoping that the family meeting would take a really short time, the same way everything in our family does. I mean, we once went on an annual family holiday that lasted from one in the afternoon until seven that night. If an affectionate hug lasts longer than three seconds in our family then everyone just assumes that the hugger's hair must have got tangled in the huggee's buttons.

Yep! Everything in our family lasts a really short time. In our family we consider the act of standing and waiting for a three-minute egg to boil to be a long-term relationship, so you can imagine that standing in the hall in your pyjamas eavesdropping for fifteen minutes with a cockroach against your ear seems like an absolute eternity. And the worst thing is that I'm really starting to need to go to the toilet and our sex-ed teacher told us that as soon as you need to go to the toilet you're supposed to go because otherwise ... Well I can't remember what happens if you don't. Maybe you explode! But anyway, my point is that I know that I should go to the toilet but I also know that I should keep standing here to eavesdrop because the longer I stand here the more sure I feel that I should be prepared for whatever it is my family's planning.

Actually now that I think about it I probably really should have been 'prepared for my family' full stop. Yep, I should have been psychologically prepared for them before I was born.

I mean, when you think about it, parents at least have the opportunity to go to birthing classes before they have a kid, and they can read books and watch videos and gasbag with other oldies to prepare. But what chance do kids have to psychologically prepare for the horrors that lie ahead after they're born. What chance does a kid have to prepare when it's only given nine months locked in a womb to prepare for a life that will last eighty years? I mean, people train for longer than that for a running race that lasts less than ten seconds.

But then again, even if I had to read a 'Prepare To Be Born' book while in my mother's womb, which probably also has shaggy carpet, there's no way in the world that it could possibly have got me mentally in tune for living with the seven aliens that masquerade as my family. How can anything prepare you for two sisters who look and act like the children of gorillas that have mated with lizards? How could anything prepare you for living with a mother whose major claim in life is that she can make a rissole out of cornflakes? How can anything prepare you for a father who once a week plays golf without golf clubs (because it's so much safer).

To be perfectly frank I'm amazed that I've grown up to be so extraordinary, particularly considering the profound lack of assistance I've received every step of the way from my family. I mean sure, they have perhaps tried in their own special way, but some times trying in your own special way just isn't enough. For example, who can forget the time they came to the school swimming carnival with a massive homemade thirty metre long sign that said 'Go Poopsy Fleur, go like the Poopsy'? Surely this was embarrassing enough, but it got worse when a wind picked up and the sign blew away, wrapped itself tightly around the principal's head and suffocated him to death.

See what I mean? I possibly could have actually won that event if my family hadn't tried to support and encourage me and ultimately caused the event to be cancelled (forever).

Oh, woe is me,

Dear Diary,

I'm still standing in the hallway with the Tupperware container pressed against my ear, but I notice now that even the cockroach seems to have passed out with boredom. Actually, I find that a bit offensive. How dare that cockroach do that? I mean, it's one thing for me to find my family dull, but it's quite another thing for a cockroach to think it too. Who is this cockroach, anyway? How interesting is it? What has this cockroach ever done for anyone else? What entertainment has it ever brought? Yeah, okay, my sister Bum Face thinks that he's her boyfriend, but it's not like they go to the movies together, or the cockroach writes poetry for her, or takes her out to dinner, or invites her dancing, or organises picnics in the park!

Yeah, so take that, Mr Cockroach and wake up!

## 7.42 am
### Still standing in the hallway

Dear Diary,

I read in a magazine somewhere about a guy who robbed a bank in broad daylight because he thought he was invisible. (Coincidentally, a couple of years ago my grandma did exactly the same thing.)

I wish I were invisible right now so that I could sneak into the living room and hear my family's plans for my birthday.

Actually, NO I DON'T. That would be a complete waste of invisibility. If I were invisible I would use my gift to secretly clean the houses of the needy, I would help the elderly cross the road without embarrassment, I would give lonely people affectionate hugs ... and then I would spend every second of my remaining time rotating my finger inside Miss Priss's ear. So no, I mean yes, I withdraw my comment about sneaking into the living room, because no matter what else I did while invisible I would not spend my invisibility listening to a bunch of escapees from the zoo discuss the fact that surprise parties are dangerous because three years ago one was held for two hundred year old Aunty Dezlee and she got such a surprise she died.

Sucked in, I say.

**7.46 am**

Dear Diary,

Well this has been pleasant, NOT. Four more minutes I've been listening through the wall and not only have I learnt nothing about my surprise party but I need to go to the toilet so badly that I actually don't think I can walk to the bathroom.

**7.47 am**

I've decided to slide down the hall to the bathroom on my bum. That way I can keep my legs crossed, not make much noise and still suppress my need to pee.

If only I had a really long skinny bendy jar then I could keep listening while I slid to the loo.

### 7.49 and a half am

The nightie Mum made for me using Christmas decorations keeps getting tangled round my waist. I'm sliding but it's taking longer than I expected.

### 7.51 am

Yep, it's taking much longer than I expected.

### 7.52 am

I think my bum is wearing away as a result of all this sliding.

### 7.53 am

Uh oh, I think my bum has disappeared! It feels like my bum's been completely rubbed off.

*7.54 and a quarter am*

Oh well, never mind, maybe old double-bummed Bum Face can lend me one of hers.
  Brilliant,

*7.54 and a half am*
*Sliding down the hall*

Dear Diary,
  Sadly, this method of transport is proving to be far too slow and I'm not going to make it to the bathroom before 'a little accident' occurs which, ironically, would mean I wouldn't need to go to the bathroom anymore. At the moment, because I've only really moved about three centimetres in all this time I am actually closer to the front door than the bathroom so I've decided to just get up and run as fast as I can into the garden.

**7.55 am**

I hope I can still run without a bum.

**7.55 and a half am**

Actually, I hope I can still pee without a bum.

Wish

me

luck.

**7.58 am**

Dear Diary,

**Bravo! I can run! I feel wild, I feel free, I feel like Kate Winslet in** *The Titanic* (when she was standing

on the bow of the ship, not when she was freezing to death in the waters of the Arctic Ocean while lying on a cupboard door).
  Love,

**7.59 am**
*In the garden*

Dear Diary,
  Okay, I'm now out in the garden and squatting by the wall of the house. I've had to be very careful of bugs, spiders, pointy sticks and pooh from the neighbour's dog, but I think I have been quite successful in avoiding all four. I'm particularly conscious of ticks because my grandma once went to the toilet while she was on a bushwalk and a tick attacked her private bits. Legend has it that this may be why she's a nymphomaniac, but personally I can't see the connection.
  But then again, I can't see the connection between my grandma and anything sexual at all because her body looks like a sandwich bag filled with the contents of a pub raffle meat

40

tray. Although I guess compared to the rest of my family, maybe you could say that my grandma is sexy because the rest of my family have bodies that look like sandwich bags filled with snot. Yes, it's true. They're all sort of beige and blobby, and in winter they go green and in springtime when the allergies arrive they all run everywhere.

Actually that bit isn't true. To be honest, it isn't even very funny. I only said that because I'm trying to distract myself from the fact that I just heard a strange crunching sound and it occurred at exactly the same time as I was lowering myself to squat and getting ready to pee. So this sound means that either something enormous is approaching or else my bum crack just got bigger.

Yikes,

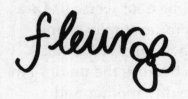

**7.59 *and a bit am***

Dear Diary,
Okay, I'm frozen in the squatting position waiting to hear another sound. I should point

out that even though I'm squatting I'm being very discreet. I'm making sure that absolutely no-one could possibly see absolutely anything that they absolutely shouldn't be seeing because the last thing I want on the day my first hit single reaches number one is to have a photo of my bottom appearing on the cover of a gossip magazine under the headline *What a Cracker!*

I am aware, however, that while I'm squatting here I look sort of like a frog that's ready to leap. I don't know why I've decided to freeze in this position. I think that perhaps it makes me feel like I'm ready for action, but considering that my enormous parachute pyjama undies are around my ankles the only situation I'm actually ready for is gross humiliation.

Actually things could be a lot worse. If I was wearing normal undies for example, people might actually see my bottom. But I'm not wearing normal undies because the undies I'm wearing were knitted by my mother and they've got this special sort of press-stud lap-lap accessory that hangs from the elastic that goes round your waist, and sort of flaps down the front and the back. The pyjama undies were inspired by an ancient *Women's Weakly* article that Mum found in the waiting room at the doctor's when she had an appointment to get three unsightly extra toes amputated from her right elbow. The magazine had seven patterns for exciting things to knit to spice up your marriage, all inspired by the American Indians and a ball of wool. Other patterns, beside the lap-lap pyjama pants, included a cape with a design of a dead bear knitted into it, shoes that doubled as canoes, a hat that attracted eagles and a little tepee that a man could put on his front bottom to keep it warm in winter.

My mother made the lap-lap undies just before she married my dad because she thought they'd be a bit of a turn-on for their wedding night (even though they actually made my mum look like an elephant in a nappy).

But anyway, I don't want to talk about sex. There's just too much of it everywhere. Well not in our house. There's none going on here, not even by my grandma! Normally she's off chasing anything with facial hair, but now she's not into it at all and I don't know if it's the result of her old age and her death-defying illness, or the fact that one month ago she accidentally mistook the bearded lady from the circus for a bloke and ended up being shot out of a cannon by the bearded lady's husband.

Grandma likes to 'get a bit' or 'do it', as she calls it, but my mother doesn't 'do it' with her husband, the Pip, because she's allergic to him, and my father doesn't 'do it' with his wife because she looks like a floor mop in a frock. And the closest Dwayne and I ever got to sex was sitting together on the same couch and watching a documentary on the mating habits of some sort of spider. In the beginning I thought the documentary was completely depressing because even though the bugs were planning on having sex there was no dating, no movies, no dinner and no prezzies. But in the last scene, after they'd 'done it' I felt strangely inspired and invigorated because the female spider bit the male's head off. I told Dwayne how fabulous I thought this was and before you know it, after the foot bandaging incident and the rumour about kissing Balderzak, he was walking through the wall.

Now I don't know if he was scared that I was going to bite his head off or if he just needed to be alone to let out all the farts I've made him bottle up since we first met, but anyway he's gone.

Oh boo hoo, boo hoo, boo hoo
booh boo hoo boo hoo, boo hoo
booh boo hoo boo hoo, boo hoo

booh boo hoo boo hoo, boo hoo
booh boo hoo, boo hoo, boo hoo
booh boo hoo, boo hoo, boo hoo
booh boo hoo, boo hoo, boo hoo
booh boo hoo, boo hoo, boo hoo
booh boo hoo, boo hoo, boo hoo
booh boo hoo, boo hoo, boo hoo
booh boo hoo, boo hoo, boo hoo
booh boo hoo, boo hoo, boo hoo
booh boo hoo, boo hoo, boo hoo
booh boo hoo, boo hoo, boo hoo
booh boo hoo, boo hoo, boo hoo
booh boo hoo, boo hoo, boo hoo
booh boo hoo, boo hoo, boo hoo
booh boo hoo!

Actually, I don't really mind.
I love Dwayne, but I don't need to own him.
I want him to be happy, I want him to be
fulfilled, I want him to be completely himself.

And you know what they say: 'If you love someone set them free!!!!!!!!!!'

But I do sort of wish he could be like a homing pigeon and find his way back to me.

Love,

**8.02 am**
*Still squatting*

Dear Diary,

Isn't this the longest squat before a pee in the entire world?

**8.02 and a half am**

I'm just squatting here looking around.

**8.02 and three quarters am**

Oh, I just saw a pillow and sleeping bag over near the shrub dad pruned in the shape of a shrub. I wonder if they belong to one of

Grandma's boyfriends.

How gross,

**8.03 am**
**Still squatting**

Dear Diary,

I'm still squatting but now I'm also
thinking about what it's like to be single.
To be honest, things haven't been nearly as
groovy as I thought they'd be for me back
out on the singles scene. I mean, so far the
only date I've had has been one that came
in a packet of mixed fruit and nuts. I've gone
with Lurline to hang out at the mall a bit,
but the only male attention we got there was
from the security guard who busted Lurline
for allegedly trying to steal a roll of toilet
paper from the toilets. (Lurline, of course,
wasn't trying to steal the roll at all and
clearly can't be blamed for the simple fact that
one end of the roll got caught in her undies
and the rest just followed her out into the
food court.)

And you know what? There isn't really anyone I want to go out with instead of Dwayne. Of course I wouldn't mind a date with Robbie Williams, or Craig David, or Heath Ledger, but that would just be so that they could remind me of my innate beauty and fundamental irresistibility, because I don't seriously want to spend much time with the sort of blokes every girl wants to get off with! No way! The situation is too threatening, too dangerous for the soft-hearted, too likely to have me ending up on the *Jerry Springer* show under the heading *This Bitch Ho Gone Green*. I want to be with the slightly ugly guys with a quirky sort of charisma that not many women can pick up on. Like Woody Allen for example, only about two hundred years younger.

Woody Allen's Best Friend

So anyway, as you can see, dear Diary, with Dwayne gone there isn't really anyone else I want to fall in love with or kiss, or whose nose blackheads I want to affectionately squish. I actually suspect that in losing Dwayne a part of me has died. In fact the loss feels quite similar to the time I was responsible for the class pet mouse over the school Easter holidays in Year Three and it was killed by one of Grandma's burps.

**8.04 am**

Dear Diary,

I was just about to start peeing but then I heard the noise again so I'm still in the frozen-squat position. I'm not going to move because I'm scared of getting busted, so all I can do is squat here and hide, and think about Dwayne and the mouse and my grandmother's burps. Oh no, now I feel quite sad.

You know, I've been sad quite a bit lately. My mother caught me crying about Dwayne in the bathroom the other day but she thought I was upset because my bosoms were growing too big. I hadn't actually thought about my bosoms being too big until my mother pointed this out, so then of course I got depressed about my bosoms *and* Dwayne. Anyway, I spent the next two days trying to bind my bosoms the way Chinese women used to bind their feet to stop them growing, but my reduced ability to breathe in and out caused me to collapse in a pile on the living room floor, where my grandmother promptly put a towel over me and used me as a footstool.

I realised later that I shouldn't have taken the bosom comment too seriously because my mother is so straight that she thinks it's scandalous to even show your earlobes in public and if she tells you that your bosoms are getting too big, then it could simply mean that you're just growing up and your bosoms are no longer dents in your chest. Later I told Mum that I wasn't depressed about my bosoms and so she told my father that I must be constipated.

Anyway, where was I? Ah yes, where I am, waiting to pee in the garden wearing a tinsel nightie and knitted lap-lap pyjama undies.

La-de-da,

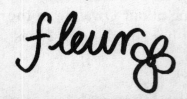

*8.14 am*
*Still squatting etc.*

Dear Diary,
   I just want to take a moment to tell you that I do realise this peeing episode is taking a rather long time, but I would also like you to know that it's taking even extra time because I'm writing everything down especially for you so that you can share the experience.
But I guess now that I've taken the time to tell you that, this peeing episode has now taken even longer. Never mind, forget I wrote that and give me back six seconds of my life. Actually, forget I wrote that last bit about giving me back six seconds of my life and give me back seven seconds of my life. Actually, forget I wrote that bit about giving me back seven seconds of my life and give me back eight seconds of my life. Actually, forget the whole thing and just buy me a finger bun.

*8.16 am*

Dear Diary,
  Okay. There hasn't been another crunching sound so I'm relaxing a bit now and getting ready to actually pee, rather than just squatting like an angry goat in anticipation of peeing.

*8.16 and a bit am*

Okay, I just heard another crunching sound. This is a bore because now I'm going to have to kill some time again while I wait for the noise to go away.

*8.16 and two bits am*

I guess I'll try killing the time by thinking just like I did a few minutes ago. Wow, who would have thought that I'd find myself thinking on purpose twice in one day! I wish I had a witness here because then they could tell my headmistress and disprove her theory that I never think at all! (No actually, on second thoughts, I don't wish that I had a witness here, because let's face it, I'm squatting in a lap-lap in the garden.)

You know, these undies aren't the first thing my mother has ever knitted for me. When I was seven she knitted me a dog. Of course it couldn't do many tricks except play dead but I really, really loved it and we got on so well that my mother also knitted me a five-year-old brother called Nat. Unfortunately, however, the neighbour's cat grabbed Nat by the 'boy bits' one day and unravelled him in a fever of chaos. So now my little brother has been reconstructed as a serviette-sized rug and can be found on the tray at the bottom of the budgie's cage. So he's not called Nat anymore and goes by the name Mat instead.

Please Note: The budgie is also knitted.

My mother knits so much for two simple reasons:

1/ because she is quite an agitated person and needs something to do with her hands. (By this I mean that if she didn't knit then my mother would have chewed her fingernails down so low that she wouldn't have any fingers.) And,

2/ because she's financially tight. Oh yes, my mother is completely unwilling to buy anything that she considers you could possibly make for yourself, and that's why our house not only contains knitted doonas but knitted towels, carpets, wardrobes, toilet paper and occasionally steak.

For a while there we also had knitted toothbrushes and toothpaste but the headmistress reported my mother to the Department of Health during a routine school dentist visit. They made my mum start buying proper dental hygiene stuff and forced her to take us to a proper dentist for a full check-up. We went, of course, because we were forced to, but when it came to payment time, Mum knitted them the cheque.

C'est la vie,

**8.17 am**

Dear Diary,

I guess you may be wondering how I'm still managing to write in you considering my current squatting position. Well the answer to this is four years of gymnastics from the age of five to nine. Oh yes, there was actually a time when I thought I might like to be an Olympic gymnast but the powers that be decided that this wasn't a good idea ... apparently due to my height, my weight and my 'profound lack of talent'.

# Profound lack of talent!!!!

Can you believe it? If only they could see me now! Actually it's probably best they don't see me now because I just peed a little bit on my lap-lap. Luckily the 'wool' Mum used is entirely synthetic and completely non-absorbent so the pee just ran off the lap-lap ... and onto my foot. Oh gross!

(Well one thing's for sure, I won't be telling Prince Charming about that should he just happen to turn up this morning to fit the golden slipper!)

**8.19 am**

Dear Diary,

You know, I've just realised this position is fantastic, because now I can pee and eavesdrop at the same time! You see, I'm right under the living room window and even though I'm making a very loud sort of whoosh-splatter sound I can pretty well make out everything my family is saying in their meeting. Ah yes, I can hear the Pip snoring (oh no he's not, that's just the way he breathes) and I can hear Miss Priss farting (oh no she's not, that's just what she sounds like when she talks) and I can actually ... no I don't think I can actually understand what they're saying because I thought my mother just said something about a television crew!

I can only imagine that when my mother refers to a television crew she is actually referring to herself holding the video camera and my father holding the microphone which is strapped on the end of a broom handle.

Oh no, they must be planning to film my birthday party! This is absolutely gob-smacking! I mean, the occasion is going to be embarrassing enough without having video evidence. Well I guess I should look at this situation through positive eyes and realise that at least I can destroy the video after it's made.

Actually, wait just one minute there ... Our family doesn't own a video camera and we certainly don't own a microphone (although we do own a broom handle). So Mum can't be talking about a crappy home video. I remember my father, under my mother's guidance, did try to make a video camera once using a shoe box and an old scooter wheel, but other than that the closest our family has ever got to a home video was showing our slides projected on the wall really, really fast.

So my response to this TV crew news is shock, horror and appallination (which is a new word I've invented that means 'as appalled as an entire nation').

I really should clean my ears,

**_8.19 and a bit am_**

Dear Diary,

Oh no, this is worse than worse, this is disastrous, because I was hoping that I didn't hear my mum talk about a television crew, because now that I think about it, the shooting of the video must require the involvement of 'outsiders'.

Yes, outsiders!

Oh, what a disaster!

You see, one of the only reasons I've continued to be able to breathe in the presence of my family for my whole life is the simple fact that I have been comfortable with the knowledge that having methodically cut out my head from all family photos and studiously liquid paper-changed the parental names on my birth certificate to Russell Crowe and Danielle Spencer, the only thing I need to do to make the removal from my martian 'family' official is to change my surname by deed poll from Trotter to Crowe. But now my devious and brilliant plans have been cruelly thwarted by the whim of my selfish mother who not only wants to video a birthday party in which, without doubt, the only highlight will be the birthday cake accidentally blowing up, but she also wants to invite someone who actually does own a video camera so that *they* can record my humiliation. And then I can't destroy the video, BECAUSE THE ORGINAL WILL BELONG TO THIS SO-CALLED 'SOMEONE' ELSE.

Well I don't want witnesses. I don't want people recording evidence! But the problem is that if Mum's already referring to them as the TV crew then it sounds like they've already been organised and hired.

Think.

Think.

Think.

Well, if we have to have them here recording then one thing's for sure — there is no way in

the world I can even smile a teensy weensy bit,
because that will ruin the theory that I live with
this family because they kidnapped me at birth.


## 8.20 am

I just heard another crunching sound. I hope it
isn't the neighbour's massive one-legged
Rottweiler.


## 8.20 and a half am

Shshshshshshshshshshshhshshshshhshsh!


## 8.21 am

No more crunch sounds, but a slight nattering
of my teeth because my bum is getting cold.
I know you're probably thinking that if your
bum's getting cold you should cover it up, but
the problem is I don't want to make any
unexpected movement when there's the
danger of a prowling one-legged giant
Rottweiler in my vicinity.
   Oh well, nothing to do but continue
eavesdropping.

## 8.21 *and a half am*

Call me mad, call me crazy, call me absolutely divine but I think my father just mentioned something about getting paid for the video. Oh no!!!!!!!!!!!!!! Surely my family wouldn't be crass enough to enter my birthday footage in some sort of funniest home video competition?

Who am I kidding? Of course they would! This family invented the word 'crass'. This is the family that has a fountain sculpture in the front garden of my parents playing Twister with no clothes on. This is the family that sent a pair of lap-lap undies to the Pope on the celebration of his eighty-second birthday.


## 8.22 *am*

I just heard another crunch sound! Shut up crunch sounds, you're interrupting my eavesdropping! Now I don't know if my mother just said that 'the TV crew is arriving today' or that 'tonight's dinner will be hay'.

Who knows?

*8.22 and a bit am*
*Still in the garden*

Dear Diary,

   Okay, I'm pretty sure that she said the TV crew will be arriving today. But why are they arriving today? It's not my birthday for ages. Why are they coming here? What do they want? Perhaps this has absolutely nothing to do with my birthday. Perhaps I should have attended the family meeting after all instead of standing outside with a cockroach container pressed against my ear and just assuming that they were discussing my birthday. I mean, now that I think about it, why would my family do anything special for my birthday? Why would they celebrate it by giving me a shock when they're all still in shock after my birth?

   Oh silly me. Oh silly billy miraculous me. Guess it's time to stop eavesdropping and do up my lap-lap ...

   Oh no, another crunch sound. No, correction, another crunch, crunch sound. Shut up crunch, crunch sound!!! My mother is saying something very important, and considering it's the first time she's ever done that in her life, I think we at least owe her the respect of listening.

   Ooops, I just farted.

Another crunch, much closer this time, a bit of a bite on the bottom from a high-jumping ant, and a family cheer as it sounds like older sister Miss Priss has just announced that she's going to read out loud from a letter.

# What!

Surely the ant bite on my bum has made me delirious because I was positive that Miss Priss couldn't read. In fact, I distinctly remember seeing her last English exam in which she'd been asked to compare and contrast the symbolism of two Shakespearean sonnets and she'd written absolutely nothing at all and instead drawn a rather colourful picture of a donkey wearing a sunhat.

And what's more, what letter could she possibly have to read? And what's more more, why in doodle-do land is she reading it *now*? Is this letter relevant to the situation? Come to think of it, is *Miss Priss* relevant to the situation? Come to think of it even more, is Miss Priss relevant to *any* situation? I say not. I say let's evict Miss Priss from the house. I say let's send her back to where legend has it she came from (a tiny butcher's shop in Dundillywa which sold small children as pet food). I say let's burn the letter that she wants to try to read because it's probably just some weird little pamphlet she found in the letterbox advertising relationships for sad and lonely people!!!!!!!!!!!!!!!!!!!!!!!

Actually now that I think about it, this pamphlet might be just what I need, because as you know I've been feeling a bit sad and lonely lately. Maybe we should let her try to read it after all.

I'm so nice and kind,

**8.23 and a bit am**

Dear Diary,
Sounds like she's reading it with or without my permission.

'And so it is with great pleasure, dear Trotters, that we announce your family as the winners of Channel Nought's International **Live with an Ordinary Family Competition** in which our camera crews move into your house for one week and film your ordinary lives. This program will be broadcast from your home, right across the globe, twenty-four hours a day for seven consecutive days.'

Please Note: We interrupt this reading to let you know that my whole family just said, 'Ooooooooooooh!' But now Miss Priss is continuing to read.

'Now that your family has been officially chosen you will soon be playing against one another for the chance to win one million dollars.'

Please Note: We interrupt this reading to let you know that my whole family just said, 'Ooooooooooooh! Aaaaaaaaaaaaaaaaaaa!' But now Miss Priss is continuing to read.
Please Note: We interrupt this interruption to let you know that my whole family just said absolutely nothing but I've just made a sort of squeaky gasping sound, a bit like a car running out of petrol or a bit like a pig after a bale of hay has fallen on its head. And now Miss Priss is continuing to read.

'The program is to be called **Trotting with the Trotters** and will involve a crew of cameramen and sound recordists unobtrusively moving into your house and subtly blending in with your day-to-day existence to observe the natural behaviour of the soon to be intergalactically recognised **Trotters**. We will let you know the rules of the million-dollar play-off within the first few minutes of the program going to air.

Good Luck,

*Anonymous*

Executive Producer

Channel Nought

The World'

This is so ... Oops I just heard another crunch, much closer this time. Oh no, now I can hear some talking and it sounds like it's right behind me. I've probably been busted by the neighbour because I think the wee dribbled backwards over some rocks and went underneath their fence.

## 8.24 and a half am

I would suspect that now is definitely the time to stop squatting. I can hear the crunching coming closer.

And closer!

### 8.24 and a half and a smidgy bit am

Okay, I'm going to get up from the squatting position now and run like the wind!

### 8.24 and two squidgy bits am

Oh no, both my legs have gone to sleep and I can't get up!

### 8.24 and three squidgy bits am

I'm stuck in the squatting position and the crunching is crunchily crunching faster and faster and closer and closer and I can't move my legs and I'm trying to fix my lap-lap.

And now a wind has picked up and my lap-lap is blowing and I'm trying to do up the lap-lap and this is absolutely the last position I want to ...

# OH NO!

## 8.25 am

A television crew has just shone a light on my backside and an interviewer has just asked my bum what my name is. (Boy, unless someone has drawn a face on my backside, I think this crew needs either a smarter interviewer or less dazzling lighting. Unless, of course, the interviewer's confused me with my sister, who you may recall is called Bum Face. Or then again, again, maybe my nickname should be Face Bum.)

## 8.25 and a humiliating bit more am

Oh, turns out the interviewer is the show's host and he has now discovered my face and told it to relax. Well isn't that a good idea, but he hasn't told me how! How am I supposed to relax while I'm squatting in the garden wearing a lap-lap? I suppose I could pretend I'm in a yoga position. But even if I do manage to convince myself that I'm a 'yellow cherry blossom about to bloom' how will I explain the lights and cameras that have suddenly surrounded me? Should I think of them as the sun and the moon?

### 8.25 *and two humiliating bits more am*

Oh great, the host guy is going to explain it all
to me. My God, he looks about as smart as a
stick. Who did his hair? It looks like grey fairy
floss. Who chose his clothes, a dead rat? I don't
think this guy is going to say anything of
value so maybe he really should be talking to
my butt because the rest of me just ain't
interested.

Love,

### 8.27 *am*

**8.29 am**


**8.31 am**


**8.32 am**
*In the bushes with the host guy*

Dear Diary,
   Sorry it took me so long to get back to you
just now, but apparently the show doesn't go
on air until 9 am so we've got a bit of time.
Anyway, the host guy did explain everything
to my face but the problem was that the
television cameras were also making the
show's opening credits, so they recorded both
the explanation and my response and

apparently I didn't look very interested in anything the host was saying to me. (I wonder why? Could it be the Face Bum thing?) So anyway, we recorded take after take after take after take until finally the cameraman asked if we could please get an actor in to play my part. But it was during this conversation that the host revealed they couldn't possibly get an actor to play my part because this was a reality TV show and if they'd wanted someone who was attractive and interesting and talented then they would have got them in the first place. (Personally, I of course found this comment a little distressing but I think the host meant it as a form of flattery.) Anyway, in Take 17 they decided to shoot the back of my head listening to the front of the host's head and apparently the back of my head looked very interested.

But meanwhile the front of my head was in shock as I listened to the host, whose name by the way is Dick Witt. As he told me a bit about the game and prepared to tell me the rules my eyes began to roll with shock and I'm pretty sure that I developed a chest rash from stress. And it wasn't because of what he was saying — it was the fact that it was him who was saying it. I mean Dick Witt looks like a piece of sushi, and he smells, and as he talks he sweats, and to be honest, the mere thought of being in his close proximity makes me want to pass out with absolute revulsion.

In fact I think I will pass out.


### 8.33 am

I just fainted but it didn't help me at all because now Dick Witt has decided to tell me all the rules and stuff *again* and he's asked me to faint *again* but this time, before I plummet to the ground, he wants me to spontaneously yell, 'Oh my God, I think I'm going to pass out with shock, horror and joy.' I'm supposed to do this after Dick tells me how lucky my family is to win this competition and how much money one of us can win if we triumph in the challenges that are going to be set before us.

This show sounds like a cross between *Survivor*, *Wheel of Fortune* and *Teletubbies*.

I think I'll just pass out again.


### 8.33 and a bit am

Okay, well that didn't work too well because even though my passing-out looked real (because it was real), Dick has ordered me to do it again because I didn't say, 'Oh my God, I think I'm going to pass out with shock, horror and joy.'

## 8.33 and two bits am

Oh my goodness gracious me. This is really hard. Fainting one minute, making the back of my head look interested the next. And now I'm meant to faint and talk and move at the same time!!!! How, I ask you, am I supposed to know how to do that? I'm not a qualified actor, I haven't done any acting classes. I mean, of course there's the chance that I'm a natural actor but I need time to focus, I need time to imagine I'm a sparrow flying through a cloud, I need time to melt like an iceblock in the summer. I need time to get a hairdresser and a make-up artist and a stylist and a therapist!

And even with all those things I don't know that I can play the part properly because the thing is that parts of my lap-lap still aren't pulled up and my circulation is now zero from squatting for so long and each time I fall to the ground I'm like a turtle on its back struggling to get up. I'm like a dog pooh just lying here on the ground. I'm like a dog pooh waiting to get trodden in and then walked through someone's house where they'll curse and swear and try to rub me off the carpet but the pong will linger for days, perhaps weeks and no matter how hard I try to be the nicest, kindest, sweetest bit of dog pooh in the world, I will still always be a dog pooh.

I've decided to tell Dick Witt he can stick his show up his left nostril.

### 8.34 am

I just told Dick Witt that he could stick the show up his left nostril and he said, 'Perfect, that's a bought one.' Which apparently means 'We just filmed you getting angry with the host and have decided to use it as the opening credits for the show **Trotting with the Trotters**.'

Fabulous? Not! Because he apparently also recorded me mumbling that stuff about being a dog pooh.

Can you believe this? We all know that other than the money, the fame and the personal sense of achievement gained after being under international scrutiny by the entire world for seven days, the absolutely other great reason for being on intergalactic television is the chance to advertise for a new boyfriend. I mean with this sort of exposure I could reach every cute dude in the world and what has my opening line of self-promotion been?

'I am a dog pooh!'

Oh, I think I'm going to pass out again.

And again.

**8.36 am**
*Inside the house*

Dear Diary,

Okay, it would appear that the TV crew has carried me inside because I am now lying on the floor of the living room secretly writing in my diary while surrounded by my 'family' and a subtle unobtrusive film crew of about a million people. Everyone is looking at me and I feel like the wild pig they chased through the forest and successfully slaughtered. Thank heavens I'm keeping this thought to myself and I'm not even mumbling it, because otherwise all any of my beloved future boyfriends would know of me is that:

1/ I am a dog pooh, and

2/ I am a slaughtered pig.

Anyway, from down here on the floor I can see that the cameras are rolling. I can also see that my 'family' must have been given a few minutes to run and prepare themselves for a week of being televised because everyone in my 'family' has changed into their very best outfits. Oh yes, my two sisters, Miss Priss and Bum Face, are wearing the matching bolero and flared-short ensembles that my mother made for them using old toilet paper rolls, and someone looks like they're wearing a dead cow ... Oh no they're not, that's just Babette, who normally looks like a dead cow no matter what she's wearing.

The Pip has dressed up in his very best pair of pastel green shorts and it looks as though he couldn't find a shirt to match because he isn't wearing one. But don't worry, we can't see his man-boobs because the Pip has pulled his shorts up so high, they actually cover most of his chest.

My grandma is wearing a bikini, and my parents are wearing the evening gown and dinner suit that my mother made out of bubble wrap for their wedding two hundred years ago. According to the photos, these outfits still look pretty much the way they did on that fateful day. But then why wouldn't they, when all the outfits have done for the last eternity is lie in the freezer, wrapped around a massive mullet (the fish, not the haircut).

Anyway, that's what they're wearing on their bodies, and on their faces each and every member of my 'family' is wearing an expression of absolute joy. I've never seen my 'family' look so happy and in fact if it weren't for their outfits I don't think I would have recognised them. The last occasion when I saw either of my parents look happy was in two separate photos that were taken before my parents actually met. The only time I've seen the Pip and Babette look happy was the time I perved on them through the keyhole and caught them sucking each other's thumbs in the broom cupboard. And the only time that I've ever, ever, ever seen my sisters look happy was the time ...

Actually, I've never seen them look happy.

So I guess all this raises the question of why I am the only member of my family not to be thrilled to bits to be on international TV. Well, there are a couple of reasons for this. One, of course, is that I am not the same as my so-called 'family' (just take a look at my elbows and you will see there are no extra toes growing there) and two, because they have no idea of the consequences of this sort of exposure. Strangers all over the world will look into our lives, analyse our table manners, scrutinise our morals and criticise our outfits (actually, I'll be doing that too). But they'll be free to look at our values, our hygiene habits, our interior décor, our interpersonal relationships and the fact that our car has a coat to keep it warm in winter that my mum knitted on her obviously not-that-exciting honeymoon. Complete strangers all over the world will see us cry over spilt milk, judge books by their covers and go on strike when the iron's hot. They'll see us shake hands instead of hug, they'll see my dad mow the lawn with an electric egg beater, they'll see Babette go to the toilet while standing up and they'll see the Pip use his snot as a nourishing sandwich spread. They'll see Miss Priss remove all unwanted body hair with a roll of masking tape, watch my grandma try to have sex with every male within a twelve kilometre radius of her walking frame, and catch Bum Face tongue-kiss her pet cockroach. Oh yes, that's right, they'll see all this and a whole lot more, and for what?

What will we get out of this intergalactic fame and a possible fortune? Publishing contracts, movie deals, A-list social invitations, free frocks, sponsorship agreements, modelling gigs, world travel and a million salivating boys wanting to love us ...

Actually, I'm starting to come around to the idea.

I mean, who cares if the entire world sees the real me and my so-called 'real family', because I've got a T-shirt that I inherited from my grandma when I was born that has written on the front 'I've never met these people before in my life'. It's pretty small on me now but I could wear it every single day of the filming as a sort of hat.

I should see this TV show as an opportunity, not a drawback. I should see it as a way of escaping from the caged, repressed and inhibited life that I've been forced to lead. I should see this as the opening of the golden door, the delivery of the magical key to freedom, the red carpet to the real me! I should see this as an opportunity to become everything that I've always wanted to be ... if only I could remember what that was.

Ah yes, I remember now. I want to be feminine yet masculine, powerful yet submissive, tall yet short, blonde-haired yet brunette, sexy yet sexless, curvaceous yet skinny, smart yet dumb as a dodo. I want to be a bit like Kylie Minogue meets Nicole Kidman meets Eminem meets a drag queen. I wonder if this show's got a budget for special effects?

And the more I think about it, even if I can't have all those things, even if I can't be represented on international TV as the world's most extraordinary human being, I can still be the super-dooper me that I've always wanted to be. I can climb out of my shell, I can emerge from my chrysalis, I can come out of the closet. Oh yes, I see it clearly now, this TV show will be a great opportunity for me to unpeel my banana!

Please Note: 'Unpeel my banana' is a phrase I've invented which means reveal the real me. The phrase isn't often used yet but you can rest assured that as soon as I become a global star everyone will be using it. Other catchphrases of mine which I hope to have introduced into everyday conversation include 'ploughing the field' (tidying my bedroom floor) and 'squeezing the lemons' (hugging elderly relatives).

Anyway, now that I've seen this TV show for the opportunity that it really is, I feel so free and so alive that I think I'll sing a song. But what song? What song can I possibly sing to let the world know of my talent, beauty, kindness and great ability to pash (due, as we all know, to years spent practising my technique by flossing my teeth with my tongue).

Oh yes, what shall I sing? Something by Christina Aguilera? (No, I'm wearing too many clothes to have cred.) Something by Mariah Carey? (No, it will scare small children.) Maybe I won't sing, maybe I'll just do a dance. No, I can't dance because then I'll have to get up off the floor. Unless of course I just dance while I'm still lying here ... You know, by just waving my arms and my legs around sort of like I'm a water sprinkler.

No, wait a minute, before I do anything quite so revealing I'd better see what position my undies are in.


### 8.37 *and a teeny bit am*

They're in the missionary position.

Please Note: 'Missionary position' means that they're pulled up and my bum's not showing and my lap-lap is lapping just the way it's supposed to.

Please Note: 'Missionary position' does not mean that my undies are in Africa converting indigenous people of that massive continent to Catholicism.

The good position of my undies does not

mean, however, that I'm going to do a dance because I've decided that a dance may not be recognisable as a dance if there's no music playing. In fact, I think it might just look like I'm having a sort of fit.

But that's okay, I can deal with no song and no dance, because I still feel great joy and optimism deep inside. So I've decided I'm just going to lie here and keep my eye on everything that's going on in the room. It'll be cool. I'll be like a mermaid, but without the ocean. I'll be like a fairy, but without the wings. I'll be like a stick with eyes.

Semi-groovy,

**8.39 am**

Dear Diary,

Oh my nipple ring!

Please Note: To my stepmother: Dear Babette, should I ever suddenly die and you find yourself irresistibly yet disrespectfully drawn to reading my completely and utterly private thoughts, I do not actually have a nipple ring. This is also a phrase I'm thinking of workshopping. It's to be used instead of *Oh my G\*d* or instead of *p\*\*h*.

Please Note: To my mother: I have also never used the rude word in my life and do not know what it means — although I do have a vague feeling that p\*\*h is a term of high praise for an excellent meal because I have often heard the Pip sit at the dinner table and whisper under his breath, 'You call this a simple meal, I call this p\*\*h.'

Anyway, back to my exclamation of 'Oh my nipple ring!' The reason I said this is because just as I was lying here on the floor while surrounded by a TV crew and an assortment of 'family members' dressed to look like an add for alternative tips on recycling domestic waste, lo and behold if my father didn't get all carried away with the attention, grab one of the soundmen's microphones and begin to do his impression of Tom Jones singing *Sex Bomb* while he pelvic thrusted at the camera.

Oh my goodness.

Oh! I can see the host panicking out of the corner of my eye because now the show might have to be R-rated. But personally, now that Dad's decided to carry on like this, I'm more concerned that the show's going to have to be rated V ... for vomit.

Pass me a bucket,

## 8.42 am
### In the living room

Dear Diary,

Dick Witt, the host, has just asked the cameramen to stop shooting. This interference in the flow of the allegedly 'live and uninterrupted' telecast from our house is all apparently okay, because I've just been told again that we don't officially start broadcasting the show until 9 am. This means that everything they've filmed so far is only to be used in the opening credits ... which is of course a great relief, unless the credits turn out to be more interesting than the actual show.

Anyway, I'm glad they've stopped filming for a moment because now I can breathe again without the weight of public humiliation pressing down upon me.


## 8.42 and a teensy bit am

Oh no I can't! The cameramen have refused to stop filming because their contracts say that they have to shoot everything twenty-four hours a day and their contracts started at 8.30. This is okay because no-one can see me. The floor manager who lis a woman and looks a lot like Miss Piggy just tripped over me because she's wearing sunglasses inside the house and presumably can't see a thing. The floor manager's job is to make sure everyone is in the right place at the right time ... including her. She's lying on top of me right now, but I don't mind because this means I'm sort of hidden and although I can't breathe I can continue to write at the same time.

### 8.42 and a couple of teensy bits am

Actually, it's very interesting lying here squashed, just watching, because I can quietly observe absolutely everything. For example, I can see from here that there is a designated cameraman with his own camera pointed specifically at each member of the family and I guess this is how it's going to be for the entire week. When I first realised this about a second ago, I suddenly went all shy because I was a little overwhelmed to have a whole cameraman and camera all to myself. I guess you have to realise that I'm really not used to having anyone want to actually photograph or film me because we don't really do that sort of thing in our family. In fact, most of the family photos that we have are just shots that have appeared in the paper after we've gone to collect Grandma from jail yet again.

But anyway, I now see this 'whole camera to myself thing' is a fantastic opportunity to really hog all the limelight. What I plan to do is make sure that all the footage of me is so incredibly interesting that the TV show won't want to broadcast a single minute of anyone else, and that way I'm bound to win the million bucks.

So right at this second I'm now trying to think of something to do that will be fabulous and irresistible to watch. I've thought of taking all my clothes off and singing the national anthem, but I have a feeling that might be illegal because I remember Grandma did that once at a friend's wedding and she was arrested straight after. Mind you, she was arrested by the Enviromental Protection Authority, so I think the charge had something to do with creating visual pollution.

Anyway, there must be something else I can do. But what?

Dum de dum.

Dad's still 'singing' and pelvic thrusting so there's a bit of competition for the attention already.

Woah, this is like the Dag Olympics,

*8.43 but nearly 8.44 am*

Dear Diary,

Oh, the floor manager just got off me. So now my camera can see me really clearly and I guess this means I'd better do something interesting.

But what? What on earth can I do to grab the whole world's attention when I can't cook, I can't sew and the only thing I'm apparently really good at is making up reasons for handing my homework in late.

I know, I'll dance like a garden sprinkler.

### 8.43 but even closer to 8.44 am

Oh great, the whole family has decided
to copy me and they're all dancing like
garden sprinklers too so I'm not standing out
at all.

### Very nearly 8.44 am

Dear Diary,
  Oh dear. Dick Witt has just run through the
room making a whole lot of noise. I think he
may be yelling 'Stop stop!' but it's hard to
understand him over Dad's singing.

### 8.44 am

Dick Witt is standing in the middle of the
room still yelling 'stop' but also stamping his
feet, pulling at his hair and trying to trip
members of my family over whenever they
dance anywhere near him.

## 8.44 and a squidgy bit am

Now Dick Witt has removed his shirt, trousers, undies and toupée and placed each of them over a different camera lens. This manoeuvre has definitely been remarkably successful when it comes to preventing the cameramen from filming but unfortunately it has also turned Grandma on to the point of hyperventilation and she is currently yelling at Dick Witt, 'Give me mouth-to-mouth or I will die.'

He, of course, is ignoring her so now Grandma has just threatened to sue him if she dies.

## 8.44 and two bits am

Oh this is terrible! My brilliant garden-sprinkler dancing has been completely upstaged by my old bag grandmother just lying on the floor. Dick Witt is calling for medical assistance on his mobile. He's explaining the situation to the ambulance driver and before you can say, 'My goodness why are you wearing protective spacesuits and full face helmets?' two ambulance men have rushed into the house wearing protective

spacesuits and full face helmets. They've
obviously heard a bit about my grandma
because although they are resuscitating her by
forcing air into her lungs, they're doing it with
a bike pump.

Clever guys,

**8.46 am**

Dear Diary,
It's weird, you know. Not long ago
Grandma was off men. (Remember? After
she was shot out of the cannon?) But now all
of sudden she's desperate to have any bloke
at all let her play with his cannon. (I don't
mean that to sound as rude as it does. But it's
true anyway.)
But enough about my grandma. What about
me? What am I thinking? What am I feeling?
Well, I'm feeling like I should think of
something really profound ... but for some
reason all I can think of is canned pineapple.
I'm also lying on the floor. I don't feel like
passing out anymore but I find this is the

best position for me to be in at the moment because not only does lying down make my stomach look really flat, but being spread-eagled in the middle of the floor means I can still make sure that even though my grandmother is in the corner getting mouth-to-mouth from a bicycle pump, I am still managing to be the centre of attention.

I'm also ensuring that I stay the centre of attention by making the sound of a soft kookaburra laugh while I stare at my camera. Not long ago this camera had a pair of men's underpants draped over the lens, but I removed them by reaching up with my toe in the middle of a sprinkler whirl when I was dancing.

You see, my new aim is to use the time before we actually go to air to make sure that my cameraman gets footage of my great array of talents, one of which just happens to be imitating a baby kookaburra. (Lots of people can't make this sound but it comes quite naturally to me because I spent about a month after I was born living with a family of kookaburras in a tree in the backyard while my mother finished decorating my nursery in a country theme using old egg shells, lawn clippings and a tractor wheel she found on the freeway.)

Oh yes, I did. Oh yes, she did.

Love,

*8.47 and a half am*

Dear Diary,

I've just realised that the host must be nude if he took all his clothes off to cover the various camera lenses, and I'm very surprised that I didn't notice this before. I mean, you'd think that most people would notice if there was a skinny nude man with a grey ponytail and a bald patch walking round their living room, so I wonder why I didn't. Maybe I didn't realise he was nude. Maybe I just assumed he was wearing a long white hairy skin-tight bodysuit because my mother knits suits just like that for a couple of her friends who like to go to noodie beaches but don't want to get sunburnt.

Please Note: I know it's hard to imagine my mother knows anyone who is so outrageous that they would even contemplate going to a beach full of naked people, but they don't actually tell my mother that they're going to a noodie beach, they just tell her that they're so modest that they don't feel quite covered up when they wear their clothes and would like an extra layer of protection.

Actually, it probably doesn't matter now whether Dick has any clothes on or not because, as I lie here making the soft kookaburra noises, I have just noticed his shadow running from the room, and unless he's had his shadow surgically removed, I assume he must have run out of the room with it.

What a dag,

*8.53 am*

Dear Diary,

I wonder why Dick Witt just ran out of the room. I wonder what's going on. I must find someone to ask. I don't feel like lying on the floor anymore but I do feel the

dramatic need to understand what shape
this show is going to take, how it's going
to be perceived, what people all over the
world will be thinking of us, and if they will
understand our complexities, our yearnings,
our desires, our potential and our belief
system. I want to know if our behaviour will
make others reassess their lives, if world
leaders will re-examine world peace, if the
hole in the ozone layer will close up, if
man's inhumanity to man will finally cease,
if child exploitation will be eliminated, if
droughts will break, if the starving will be
fed ... and if the whole world thinks that
I should change into something more
figure flattering or perhaps more brightly
coloured?

*8.55 am*

Dear Diary,
   I just asked my cameraman why Dick Witt
ran from the room and before he answered he
checked his watch. Personally I was offended

that he apparently wanted to make sure that talking to me didn't waste too much time because that's exactly what my stepfather, the Pip, does. But anyway, it turns out he was checking his watch to see if it was nine o'clock yet because apparently the crew aren't allowed to talk to us once the show starts being broadcast.

Aha! Well luckily, because it's only five to nine, he has five minutes to go into all the details. Great, I'm focused, I'm ready, I'm prepared to listen. Bring on the explanations, Mr Cameraman, because I'm ready and waiting!

### 8.55 and the smallest bit am

Well, that only took the smallest bit of time because the cameraman said he didn't know.

### 8.56 am

Now I've asked the floor manager why Dick Witt ran from the room but she isn't speaking. I'm not surprised because I think she must be very embarrassed ... She's wearing a fluorescent pink kaftan that looks like one of Grandma's and has hair that looks like road kill. Honestly, she's dressed so badly she could be one of my relatives. Anyway, she's written her answer for me and it says that Dick Witt is editing the opening credits.

This is not good news because if Dick is editing then this means that Dick is both the host and the director of this show, which means he's in control of whatever images the world gets to see of me ... which means ...

that I should have been a lot nicer to him.

Oh yes, I should have been a whole lot nicer to him because now the opening credits are just going to be a frenetic montage of my bum, me calling myself a dog pooh and a slaughtered pig, my father singing while he pelvic thrusts at the camera, my grandmother groping, the ambulance arriving, a bicycle pump and the back of my head yelling, 'Oh my God, I think I'm going to pass out with shock, horror and joy!'

FABULOUS! *NOT*!

Anyway, the hooded floor manager also wrote in the note that the show's editing will take place in a massive bus which is currently parked in our driveway. Apparently the bus has an enormous satellite dish on top of it and 'the whole vehicle is like a television studio on wheels, man!' Once the show begins this bus is basically the place where Dick will spend the entire week.

Well if he is nude I hope he doesn't catch a chill.

(Or piles.)

Love,

**8.59 and a half am**
**The show's about to go to air**

Dear Diary,

Oh my neurological cells! (And yes I do have those.) The show is going live to air in thirty seconds and I've just realised that no-one has told us what to do. I recall that when Miss Priss read the letter it said that we would be told the rules within the first two minutes of the show going to air, but I thought that was an exaggeration purely for dramatic effect. I mean, what's the point of finding out what you're doing once you're already doing it? This could be a catastrophe. This could be grossly humiliating! I know that at a time like this one needs to be strong, brave and focused, but I've decided to take an alternative course of action and to simply be pathetic.

I've decided to cling to the nearest cameraman and sob.

Sob!

**9 am**

Dear Diary,
   Nine am!!!!!!!!!!!!!!!! How did that happen?
One minute it's 8.59 and a half am and then
thirty seconds later it's 9 am! Unbelievable!
I guess they must be rolling the opening
credits by now and the cameraman will be
filming us live any second.
   Oh! The floor manager just mouthed at me
'act natural', so I've draped myself over the
arm of the couch and begun to sing *Somewhere
Over the Rainbow*.


**9 am and fifteen seconds**

Apparently they are broadcasting the opening
credits.


**9 am and twenty-nine seconds**

I've stopped singing now, because it turns out
I only know the first four words of the song.
But the good news is that now that I've
stopped singing I can hear a voice through my
cameraman's headphones. Gee, that volume
must be turned up loud! I suspect that the

cameraman is either already deaf or is about to go deaf from listening to his earphones on a volume that's too high.

But wait a minute, what am I sitting here worrying about the cameraman for? Oh this is just further evidence that I'm too kind and considerate. That is definitely something I must try to change because we all know that you never get rich by caring about the welfare of other people. Just look at Mother Theresa.

But wait another minute, because I should be concentrating on **Trotting with the Trotters** and I'm getting distracted (which is not surprising considering that both my parents have the concentration span of a mozzie and my grandma can't concentrate on anything at all unless it is a bloke).

## 9 am and twenty-nine seconds and a half

Each member of my 'family' has just been given a small microphone which we have to clip onto ourselves and wear all the time so that the TV show can record every single sound we make. Guess I know one person who won't be burping or farting for an entire week.

I hope I don't explode.

### 9 am and thirty seconds

Aaaaaaaaaaaaaaaaaaaaaaaaaaaaaaaaaagh!
Someone just yelled 'Action!'

But what does this mean? 'Action!' as in just
get on with your normal day-to-day life, as in
the Pip going to the toilet to read Enid Blyton
for two hours, Babette removing her facial hair
with an industrial vacuum cleaner, Dad
building us a plasma TV screen using an old
frame and a poster of Egypt, and Mum
cleaning the entire house by sucking the dust
up with a straw!!!!!

Or does 'Action!' mean 'Action!' as in the
cameras are rolling, the whole world is
watching, and just behave appropriately by not
doing things like picking your nose and eating
the snot? (My goodness, what will Miss Priss
and Bum Face exist on for the next week?)

I wish someone could at least tell us
what the rules are for this TV show.

*I mean what is going on here!!!!!!!!!!!*

### 9 am and thirty-one seconds and a bit

Oh! I've just realised that all of a sudden
no-one is paying me any attention. (WOW!
Flashback to the whole of my life so far. You

know even when I was born I had to type out little memos to the nursing staff and gynaecologist just to interrupt their viewing of the home shopping channel in the corner of the delivery room and let them know I'd actually arrived.)

Of course my 'family' reckons that my problem is that it wouldn't matter how much attention I received it still wouldn't be enough. But I think it's all much deeper than that and my problem is actually my 'family'. It's not that I don't love them or anything, it's just that I feel lonely whenever I'm in their company, and as anyone will tell you who's ever watched Tom Hanks in *Castaway*, loneliness can make you think that a soccer ball is your friend.

A very badly drawn
Soccer ball

Anyway no-one is paying me any attention, no-one on the TV crew and no-one in my 'family' and I'm only just managing to make my own cameraman face me. I can't imagine what else is holding their attention so firmly. Has someone dead just walked into the room? Has the cat just coughed up the knitted poncho it swallowed in 1997? Has Babette finally confessed to being the by-product of a chance meeting between a baboon and a toilet brush?

Quick, tell me,

### 9 am and thirty-two seconds

Dear Diary,

I have the answer.

It would appear that they're all paying attention to the program's host, who has apparently returned from editing the opening credits and starting the broadcasting of the show and is now standing in the doorway and laying down the rules of *Trotting with the Trotters*.

I really should listen to these rules, but before I do, dear Dairy, I would just like to spend a brief moment describing the esteemed host of this program. I'm pretty sure that he was cryogenically frozen in the early eighties. He's wearing faded, tight, waist-high jeans and really, really white runners. He has a boof of hair that is a toupée and wraps all around his head sort of like a Brussel sprout then culminates in a ponytail at the back. He speaks with a lisp and a splatter of spit in the octave range of a canary. From what I can see, he has no obvious talents or charisma ... so basically I'm surprised he's not a politician.

Anyway, enough analysis of the man who presumably will be popping in and out of our lives over the next week and on to what on earth he'll be doing when he does pop into our lives. Yes, I believe it is time for me to tune into our rules and hear how this game is to be played.

### 9 am and forty seconds

Uh, oh. Well that's a spot of bad timing, because Dick Witt has just FINISHED explaining how the game is played so now I haven't got a clue.

Help,

## 9 am and forty-two seconds

Dear Diary,

Oh no. My entire 'family' is suddenly chanting in unison 'No cheating, winners can be losers', and I have no idea what they're talking about. I mean, the last time my 'family' chanted anything it was the family motto at my grandpa's funeral and even then no-one could remember precisely if it was 'Shine light upon all those whom you pass on your path' or 'Do your best but always give up before you humiliate yourself'.

Anyway, so now my 'family' is chanting and I'm leaning on the knitted sofa trying to look focused and in control but not actually having a clue what we're trying to achieve here.

I've whispered to Miss Priss and Bum Face to ask them what the rules are but neither of them has answered. This isn't surprising. I mean, while it's possible that they're both just being incredibly rude and inconsiderate to a sister who's done nothing but support and encourage them throughout their miserable, whiny little lives, it's also possible they simply didn't hear me. You see, despite all that's happened so far, it's still the morning and in the mornings both Miss Priss and Bum Face each has a massive build-up of wax in their ear canals. Normally Mum squeezes their heads with a nutcracker to make the wax pop out, but maybe she hasn't had time to do this yet.

Please Note: My mother has trained professionally to do the nutcracker thing. I do not suggest anyone try it at home.

### 9 am and forty-five seconds

Oh, actually I've just realised that both Miss Priss and Bum Face must have lip-read me as clear as a bell because Miss Priss said that if I speak to her one more time she's going to dob on me.

# Dob on me!

Well fine, go ahead. Because if you dob on me I'm going to gob on you!!!!

Love,

## 9 am and fifty-five seconds
### Still in the living room

Dear Diary,

I've decided to ask my stepmother Babette just exactly what the rules are. I would have asked the Pip, but he's an idiot. And besides, Babette is the person sitting closest to me, she is also my stepmother, she is living in our house, she has married my dad, and I know for a fact that it is definitely her who leaves occasional hairs on the toilet seat. So I'm pretty sure that I will simply ask her for her help and she will respond positively. And if she doesn't I will offer her three dollars and then she will respond positively. And if she doesn't then I will sit on her foot and then she will respond positively. Et cetera.

## 9 am and one minute

Okay, I am currently sitting on Babette's foot and she is not responding positively. In fact, she's screaming at the top of her lungs and her cameraman is moving in for a close-up of her oesophagus.

Right, well obviously that didn't work out quite as I expected, but never mind, now that

Babette has drawn attention to the situation I'm sure that someone or other will recognise my dilemma and come forward to assist me.

## 9 am and two minutes

No-one has come forward, no-one is assisting me. No-one is doing anything except actively not talk to me.

Oh boo hoo,

## 9 am and nearly three minutes

Dear Diary,

This is ridiculous, this isn't natural. The cameras have started rolling and this is all wrong. I mean, how can anyone think that we are properly portraying my familial relation-ships if no-one is talking to me? This is not reality television. A correct portrayal of my 'family', as we all know, is absolutely the other way round ... with me not talking to them.

# How dare they!

**9 am and three minutes and seven seconds**

Oh! All the cameramen and sound men are telling me to shhh!

Aaaaaaaaaaaaagh! Go and tell yourself to shhh because no-one tells me to shhhh! Well, all of my teachers do and all of the teacher's pets do, and old people on the bus do and complete strangers in the cinema do, but other than that absolutely no-one ever tells me to shhhhhh. Certainly no-one in this room anyway.

**9 am and four minutes**

Everyone in the room just told me to shhhhh.

Oh, I feel so lost and alone. I haven't felt this lost and alone since I was lost and alone after my sisters abandoned me in the fruit section at Woolworths when I told them that I didn't think that they were really very good sisters and I would prefer to be related to a lemon and a raisin.

Raisin      Lemon      Dead Fly

But anyway, back to my dilemma, which is the fact that I don't know the rules of this game! Surely my mother will tell me the rules. Surely my father will tell me how to play this game? Surely Grandma can give me a minute of the short few minutes remaining in her life? Yes, surely she can spare a moment to talk to the only grand-daughter who has ever been brave enough to give her something for Christmas other than bath salt or talcum powder. I mean sure the toy gun I gave her last year did cause a bit of drama when she went to the bingo hall that she visits each Wednesday and shot her fish and chip lunch. But hey, who among us hasn't done that?

And sure the second-hand skateboard I gave her the year before did cause her to dislocate both her hips and end up on the side of the road resembling a blob of mashed potato. And yes, I did give her the box of magic tricks which resulted in the tragic and so far permanent disappearance of Bertold Wilson. But hey, what did he expect? I mean, the trick was called the 'Incredible Disappearing Trick'. (I think he should be grateful that Grandma didn't saw him in half!)

But anyway, yes, I did give Grandma the edible undies that nearly killed Edgar Notsbrough when his dentures got caught on one of the chewie bits and he choked and stopped breathing for two days. And yes, I did give Grandma the accelerated foot warmer that actually set her bedsocks on fire ... while she was wearing them. But at least I didn't give her bath salts. I mean, people can drown in the bath.

Can't they?

**9 am and four minutes and a quarter of a second**

Dear Diary,
Grandma won't talk to me. How rude, dude!

### 9 am and four minutes and thirteen and three-quarter seconds

Actually, maybe Grandma's not talking to me because she's dead!

No, she still has a pulse.

Maybe Grandma's pretending to be dead yet again in order to get more attention. That'd be right. What a self-obsessed person! Apparently when she and Grandpa were getting married Grandma pretended to be dead right in the middle of the ceremony because Grandpa had accidentally left his fly undone and the priest was winking at him and ignoring Grandma altogether.

### 9 am and four minutes and thirteen and three-and-a-bit-quarter seconds

Dear Diary,

Now that I think about it, pretending to be dead could be a very good way to bring the focus back to me right here and now.

Brilliant,

### 9 am and four minutes and thirteen and three-and-two-bit-quarter seconds

Okay, I'm no longer sitting on Babette's foot and am back sitting on the knitted couch but I'm no longer looking focused and in control and instead I'm trying to look dead.

### 9.05 am

I just heard Dick Witt talking through the cameraman's headphones. Fantastic! He seems to be commenting on my deadness. Great, now maybe he'll wonder why I'm dead and it will occur to him that I need attention and he'll wonder why I need attention and then he'll realise that I'm feeling lost and alone, then he'll wonder why I'm feeling lost and alone and then it will occur to him that it's because I happened to be thinking about something else at the time that the rules were being revealed. And he will then understand that this is a perfectly normal thing to do, and will almost laugh with delight as he recognises that 'not concentrating' is the sort of thing brilliant people often do, and then he'll not only tell me the rules but will perhaps nominate me as group leader.

Oh, Dick just said, 'Tell her to hold that dead pose, she finally looks presentable.'

Thank you, Dick Witt.

Very kind of you,

*9.05 am and fourteen seconds*
*Not doing anything interesting, just draped across four cushions knitted in the shape of pineapples ... very uncomfortable*

Dear Diary,

Okay, I have just had a psychic experience and I am very excited.

Dear Diary, I'm not sure if you've heard that I'm occasionally a bit psychic but I am. Actually, now that I think about it, or actually get a bit psychic about it, I realise you probably haven't heard about it because you don't have ears. So I will tell you how psychic I am. Very! A few of my aunts have been psychic as well. Aunty Gladys, for example, allegedly foresaw her own death while standing on the railway tracks only moments before she was run over by a train. Anyway,

the whole point of me telling you that I am
a bit psychic is that I've had a sudden vision
of something amazing that's about to happen
any second ... so I think I should stop writing
and wait.

*9.05 am and sixteen seconds*

*9.05 am and twenty-five seconds*

*9.05 am and thirty-seven seconds*

*9.05 am and fifty-two seconds*

*9.06 am and fourteen seconds*

Oh well, maybe I was wrong. Or maybe I was
tuned into the wrong brain channel and
something really amazing just happened on
someone else's television show. Whatever it
was, nothing amazing happened here.

Oh, that's so typical, so disappointingly predictable. I can't believe it, after all of my heavily veiled excitement, after all of my cleverly disguised enthusiasm, after all that I've secretly hoped this **Trotting with the Trotters** adventure might be, it turns out that this experience might be as flat as Miss Priss's chest. Gee, this is about as disappointing as the first time I accidentally saw Dwayne's willy and thought he was being attacked by a tiny little snake.

Bingo,

**9.07 am**

Dear Diary,

Oh well, back to our show. Where all my 'family' is sitting down in the living room with their eyes closed.

# What?

Oh, I hope their eyes aren't closed.

Surely someone should call an ambulance!

My family doesn't normally sit down with their eyes closed! My family doesn't even lie down with their eyes closed! My family doesn't sleep with their eyes closed! No-one in my family ever closes their eyes ... well maybe they used to three hundred years ago, but they certainly haven't in the recent past ... not since Aunty Pixie died while dozing when a sausage dog crawled up her nose.

Surely this can't be right? Are they tired, are they praying, are they tring to be non-threatening? Closing your eyes is dangerous! Surely a game like this TV show can't wilfully encourage people to risk their lives? Surely there should be some work-safe practices employed here. Surely if people are going to be encouraged to do dangerous things then there should be special bits of safety equipment brought into the house: fire retardant uniforms, dimmers on the light switches, eight separate sausage dog nets!

SURELY SOMEONE CAN TELL ME WHAT'S GOING ON!!!!!!

Surely the fact that I'm the only one who doesn't know what's going on here is outrageous? Surely this is exploitative? Won't someone tell me the rules? Won't someone tell me what game we're actually playing?

*A few seconds later*

Well, if no-one will tell me what the rules are then I'm just going to have to make up my own.
   Love,

*9.07 am and fifty-eight seconds*

Dum de dum
Dum de dum
Dum de dee!
Dum de dum
Dum de dum
Dum de dee!
Dum de dum
Dum de dee!
Dum de dum
Dum de dum
Dum de dee!

Well I am at a loss. I mean, the idea of creating my own rules seemed like a really good idea until I realised that my strength is not actually in creating things but knocking things down. What I need is not to create my own rules but to hear what we're supposed to be doing and then not do it. So before I don't follow the rules I need to know what they are.

But in the meantime, I tell you, if this show is being broadcast it must already be the most boring show in the world. I think someone on this show should do something interesting so that our show isn't cancelled after being on air for just five minutes and fifty-eight seconds. I mean, maybe we should spice things up by doing some live and hurried renovation of the backyard, or perhaps cooking something extraordinary using surprising ingredients, for example, vegemite with salmon.

I guess we could ask our family members various quiz questions for a million dollars but my 'family' wouldn't know any of the answers and they wouldn't be able to phone a friend, because of course they don't have any.

I suddenly feel strangely incapable of pulling this TV show thing off. I want to go home.

Oh, I am home.

Damn it,

P.S. I just realised my family members haven't closed their eyes at all. They're just trying to look seductive so they can woo the audience. My goodness, they'd have better luck doing that with a sausage dog up their nostrils.

**9 am and eight minutes**
**On the couch**

Dear Diary,
This is good, the floor manager just crawled behind the couch in her high heels and hairy feet and slipped a memo from Dick Witt into my hand. How outrageous! How illegal! How absolutely fabulous! Maybe this note will have the rules written on it. I competely can't wait to read the note but I'm just not sure how to do it while still pretending to be dead.

**9 am and eight and a half minutes**

I've decided that in order to read the note I'm going to flop off the couch and onto the floor.

While doing this I'll make sure that the lampshade that my mother made using an old bucket falls on my head after it falls off the coffee table that my father made out of an old coffee table. Once the bucket lands on my head it should cover my head completely and thus allow me to read the memo without getting busted by the cameras.

**9 am and nine minutes**

Okay, that was a good and a bad idea, because on the one hand while plummeting from the couch, rolling across the floor and skilfully managing to capture my own head in a lampshade that was formerly a bucket has meant that I can now read the memo, it has also unfortunately led to the realisation that I'm unlikely to be able to remove the bucket without the external assistance of perhaps a crane and a winch.

And to top it all off, the only two things the memo said were, 'You are now being very boring. If you are currently being yourself then try to be someone else.'

### 9 am and nine and a half minutes

I hate to tell you, but where I come from this *is* me and if the director isn't happy with it then he can stick his telephoto up his close-up.

I've decided to give up and quit this game. We're nine and a half minutes into it and I don't appear to be winning, and basically I've got better things to do with my time.

Love,

### 9 am and ten minutes

Dear Diary,

Well, I may have better things to do with my time but I also have a bucket on my head and as far as I can see, which let's face it is not very far, before I do anything I am going to have to get help. So I've decided to write 'help' on the back of the memo and hold it up in the air.

### 9 am and ten and a half minutes

That's interesting, I can feel that a swarm of presumably family and cameramen have come closer to me but no-one has actually offered assistance. I can understand the cameramen not helping because I guess they're not allowed to interfere with the activities of the house, but why isn't my family helping?

This is devastating. This is so confronting. These people are supposed to love and look after me. Family are supposed to be your friends through thick and thin, aren't they? Surely the only reason we have siblings isn't so that we can borrow their deodorant when they're not looking? And surely the only reason we have parents is not so that we have someone to escort us to parent-teacher nights! I mean, that would be ridiculous, particularly when I always hire attractive unemployed actors to play my parents at school functions.

Really, all I'm asking for is a little help here. I'm not being unclear. I'm being quite precise. I'm not mucking around with girlie-whirlie language and sulky facial expressions hoping that someone will perhaps translate my desires. I'm lying here with a bucket on my head holding up a sign that says 'help'.

**9.15 am**

I can hear Dick Witt telling the cameramen to
zoom in on me and get a close-up. So now I'm
giving the cameraman a close-up of 'the
finger'.

Fleur scores again.

Love,

**9.15 and a half am**

Dear Diary,

Wow, that's weird! A deafening siren has just
gone off and now my entire family, led by the
cameramen, are chanting 'Rule number five,
obscene gesture.' And they're telling me that
I've just lost $10,000.

Okay, that's it. I'm refusing to do a single
thing until someone tells me what's going on.

**9.33 am**

I'm waiting.

## 10.45 am

I'm still waiting.


## 11 am

Well no-one has bothered to tell me anything
so I'm thinking of ringing my friend Lurline
to ask if she's watching the TV and if she can
tell me anything about the show I'm on. I'm
fully aware that this may be a very dangerous
thing to do:

1/ because I am probably not allowed
external contact with anyone or anything for
the duration of the show, and

2/ because I'm wearing a bucket on my head
and the reverberation of my own voice is
likely to deafen me for life, and

3/ because Lurline tends to lie.

You see, Lurline is one of those people who
is absolutely hilarious to hang out with. She's
always full of side-splitting stories and
fantastic gossip but the problem is almost
none of it is ever actually true. It's like she's got
some sort of computer virus in her head that
corrupts all the facts she knows, multiplies
them by a billion, chops them into little pieces
and scatters them far and wide. I remember

when I first met Lurline she told me that her real parents were Prince William and Kylie Minogue and that she was kidnapped at birth. Oh no, wait a minute, that's the story I told her.

But nevertheless, Lurline is my best friend and I need to hear her voice. I need her reassurance that I haven't made an absolute fool of myself and that the camera lighting is flattering to my skin. I need her to help me with rules, goals and strategies. I need her to tell me how to keep my hair looking full and shiny under these intense TV conditions, and I need her to tell me how to cheat.

Lurline has always helped me in times of crisis. Actually no, she hasn't, but despite this I'm hoping that for once in my life she will be reassuring and encouraging and not say the sort of things she usually does like, 'Gee that dress makes your waist look so small. Because it makes your butt look absolutely enormous.'

An Enormous Butt

Anyway I've rolled across the floor while I've been writing and I'm over near the phone now casually getting ready to ring Lurline but I can't actually see the phone very well because I've got a bucket on my head. So first thing I have to do is remove the bucket. You know I really can't understand why it won't budge. I mean, it went on, why won't it come off? Shoes go on and then they come off, why on earth won't the bucket? And you know what's worse is that this bucket is not only sitting very snugly on my head but it's actually getting more and more snug.

Why is it getting tighter on my head? It can't be because my head is swelling with pride!

### 11 am and seventeen seconds

Oh, my golly, I've just realised it's because the pimple on my forehead must be growing! Oh my yuck, this is gross. And what's even more gross is the fact that if I'm going to have any chance whatsoever of getting this bucket off my head I'm going to have to pop that zit first.
Yuk,

## 11 am and two minutes
### Still in the living room

Dear Diary,

I'm still in the living room but now I've stolen one of my mother's knitting needles. My family still has their eyes sexily-seductively-squintily-semi-closed but the whole world can still see me so I'm trying to look completely normal poking the knitting needle up and under the bucket in an effort to locate the puss mountain.

I think I've just found it.

Ouch!!!

No I haven't, that was my eye.

Actually now that I think about it, knitting needles are incredibly dangerous and I can't believe that my parents allow them in the house. I mean, when you consider that we don't allow uncooked spaghetti in the kitchen because it's considered to be too hard and pointy, why on earth are we permitting knitting needles? I must report this to my family and if it means that my mother has her only source of joy removed from the house then so be it ... at least then she'll know how I felt when I was four and she made me dump my best friend in the universe, even though my best friend was invisible.

## 11 am and three minutes

Okay, I've located the target and poked it with the knitting needle. I know it's gross but at least no-one else knows what I'm up to and it will all be over before they find out.

## 11 am and three minutes and two seconds

Oh no, a siren has just sounded.

## 11 am and three minutes and five seconds

Oh, double no, the host has just made an announcement that I've lost another $10,000 for endangering the lives of others. How have I done that? It was my eye, my pimple, how does that endanger anyone else? It's not like there was so much puss that anyone was going to drown in it.

## 11am and three minutes and thirty seconds

I am completely sick of doing everything wrong in this game and being the one who doesn't fit in and the first chance I get

# I am quitting!

## *11 am and four minutes*

Anyway, the good news is that the bucket has slid off. YEAH!

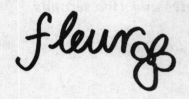 

## *11 am and four minutes and twenty seconds*

Dear Diary,
   Oh, the floor manager just ran right into my shot and shoved Mum's latest piece of craftwork on my head. It's a hollow pumpkin carved like the Sydney Opera House.
   Feeling bad,

## 11 am and five minutes

The worst thing about this is the realisation that Dick Witt the director must have told the floor manager to stick the pumpkin on my head because he thinks that I look better with it on. Thank you! But the good news is that the pumpkin hasn't gone all the way down over my face because the floor manager made sure that, a bit like a fat, hard hat, it just sat low enough to cover the explosion on my forehead but didn't cover my eyes. Basically she rested it on my ears, which was very kind and sweet of the floor manager.

So what's that about?

## 11 am and six minutes

Dear Diary,
   Now that everything's back to normal-non-normal, it's time to ring Lurline. And now that the bucket isn't covering my eyes I can see that I'm next to the phone. I can also see that for no apparent reason my family members have

131

now fully opened their eyes, so in order not to get busted by Dick Witt or my disloyal family I'm trying to act like I'm just really interested in the phone as an object — you know, like I've never actually seen a phone before and I wonder what it is and what it does. I'm acting a bit like someone from that movie *Planet of the Apes*, who's just been shown his very first wheel. (I don't mean that I'm grunting like a gorilla, I mean I'm studiously and curiously staring at the phone and holding it up to get a closer look. Please Note: I am also not scratching my fleas.)

Now, with my other hand I'm going to casually start pushing the phone buttons and then when I hear the beep sounds I'm going to giggle with delight.

## 11 am and six and a half minutes

Okay, I just did the giggling with delight thing and the floor manager seems to be aiming a paper airplane at my head.

## Midday and seven minutes

The airplane landed in my ear and I've only
just managed to successfully remove it because
the pointy bit got jammed inside my eardrum.
I think that there's a message written on the
paper and boy I hope this message is worth
reading because it's not only interrupted my
performance of 'prehistoric man discovers
talkie-talkie device', but it's also taken an hour
to extract it from my ear.

Actually, I've realised that I shouldn't
abandon my performance halfway through just
so that I can read some note that with any luck
will have the rules written on it but will more
than likely say something like 'you've got a
blob of snot the size of a small continent
hanging out of your left nostril' or 'there's a bit
of cornflake rissole on your tooth'. So I've
decided to continue my discovery of the
wonders of the telephone and casually read the
message at the same time. (But before I do this
I'm going to ever so subtly sniff as hard as I can
and casually bend down to wipe my nose on
something just in case there is a massive blob
of snot up there. I realise, of course, that it
would be wrong for me to wipe my nose on
my sleeve while on international television, so
I've decided to wipe it on Bum Face's sleeve.)

## Midday and seven minutes and twelve seconds

There, the sniffing wiping thing is now all done, but while I'm in this bending down position I've realised that I should also probably find some way to check my teeth for stray food particles. There are, as I said, no mirrors in the house, so I'm going to have to just use a shiny object. I'd use a spoon if my mother hadn't removed them all four years ago after she read an article in *Women's Weakly* about a woman who died while eating a tub of ice-cream because she accidentally ate the spoon.

## Midday and seven minutes and 53 seconds

Well the only shiny reflective object I can see in this vicinity is the Pip's bald spot, so I'm going to stop playing with the phone for a second and go and check the reflection of my teeth on the Pip's head.

## Midday and eight minutes

Okay, well I didn't see any food particles in my teeth but I did spot some massive dandruff flakes on the Pip's head and five sizeable bits of broccoli. That's interesting, because Mum and Dad haven't permitted any broccoli in this house since Dad read an article that said you could die if you ate a paddock full of broccoli every day of your entire life. So the discovery of broccoli in amidst the Pip's dandruff raises the question has the Pip been sneaking off to secretly eat broccoli or is he growing it in his head? (And if he is growing it in his head does dandruff make a good fertiliser?)

But enough of other people. Now back to something much more interesting. Me! Me, me, me, me, me! But what was I doing? Ah yes, nothing.

Oh no, that's not correct, I was actually about to read a note and check out the phone buttons at the same time. Ah, if only our headmistress could see me multi-skilling or multi-tasking or whatever multi-thing it is that I'm doing here. That'd soon prove her theory wrong about me being unable to concentrate on more than ...

Oh, I've lost my train of thought.

Anyway, I'm now back in precisely the situation I was in before I received the note in my ear and then went off to check my teeth in the Pip's reflective head. I'm pushing the buttons on the phone and giggling with childish glee. 'Tee hee, tee hee, te, heee.' I think I'm probably looking pretty good at the moment. I can feel that I've really conquered the part I'm playing here of Paleolithic woman discovering the phone. I'm giggling delightedly and I think I'll giggle some more because I'm very comfortable with the fact that it gives my acting a childish non-threatening credibility.

### Midday and nine minutes

I just read the note and it said, 'Stop giggling, you look like a drunk hyena.'

Well we'll soon see about that because I have surreptitiously dialled Lurline's number and within moments I know that she will get on the phone and tell me just how fabulous I look on TV and how she hasn't been this breathtakingly proud of anyone but herself since she gave Hindle Ringworm such a huge wedgie that he had to be hospitalised to have it removed.

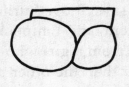

## A Huge Wedgie

*Midday and ten minutes approximately*

Okay, I just tried to stick as much of the phone receiver as possible up into the pumpkin, but only the aerial would fit. So now most of the phone is hanging down, but I hope it just looks like I've got one really low, really big, really creamy white earlobe.

*Midday and approximately ten minutes and four seconds*

Oh, Lurline's mother just answered and said that Lurline isn't speaking to anyone because she's too embarrassed by my behaviour on TV.

What! An attitude like this from a girl who's been wearing tennis balls in her bra since she was nine, judgments like this from a girl who started shaving her legs when she was three, superiority like this from a girl who wears a fake tattoo that says 'I love Lurline' and is signed by Eminem (and Eminem is spelt M&M!). All this from a girl who wears one shoe heel higher than the other just so that her bum swings more when she walks!

Well you can forget the fake-cleavage-body-paint voucher I was going to buy you for your birthday Missy Lurline Backrug.

I am so hurt. I am so alone. I am so surprised that my best friend would betray me like this. Of all people! What does she have to be embarrassed about (other than all the things I just listed above). I mean, I'm the one being embarrassing, I'm the one peeing in the garden, I'm the one with a bucket on my head, I'm the one who's taking a risk and putting herself on the line here so what right has she to lie on her puffy pink doona and ordain that she's embarrassed?

# And while we're at it, what right does a director have to tell me how to be me!

You know a moment ago I was thinking that I didn't want to be involved in this TV show but now, as far as I'm concerned this game is ON! I will be Fleur Trotter non-stop for the next seven days and I won't care what other people say or think because I'm a winner already just for daring to be me.

Trophy for Me

So now all I have to do to be truly successful is work out who 'me' is. And at the moment I only know who I'm not.

I know what I don't like. I know what doesn't make me happy. I know that I don't want to tongue-kiss Elvis Presley, even if he is still alive. But who am I, how am I defined, what do I like, what do I want?

If someone were to describe me, what would they say? If I found a description of myself on a torn page blown onto the footpath, would I read it and recognise me? Only if I'd written it (and even then I'd know it wasn't true because I'd plagiarise bits from

Fantales wrappers just to make my life sound more substantial).

Maybe Dwayne's right and I really do need to take a good, long, hard look at myself.

But then again maybe he's wrong, and I don't.


## Midday and twelve minutes

My family is chanting 'Loser! Loser!' because apparently they all realised I was talking on the phone when they saw me drop the receiver in disgust after talking to Lurline's mum and now I've just broken rule number seven by communicating with the outside world. I guess this means that I've probably lost another $10,000 but I don't care. As far as I know I only had $7.50 in the first place and even that is only a rough estimate of the coins I collected from behind the couch while I was lying on the floor with a bucket on my head.

Which reminds me, I still have a pumpkin on my head, and now would probably be an exceptionally good time to get it off because it's really hurting my ears and if I wait too long then my ears might swell to such an enormous size that they blow up like balloons and the only way I will ever be able to get the pumpkin off is if I have my ears surgically removed. And then how could I wear earrings!

  Bloody hell,

*Midday and fourteen minutes*
*Still in the living room. Still with a*
*pumpkin on my head.*

Dear Diary,

  Okay, slightly pretty bad problem. Turns out my ears haven't swelled at all and they have in fact shrunk. This has happened because the blood that normally would have circulated to my ears has not been able to reach them because of the pressure of the pumpkin. So the blood is now gathering in my head and making it expand. So the point is, if I don't hurry up and get the pumpkin off then my head will swell and swell and swell and I'll never ever be able to get the pumpkin off my head and I'll have to forget any thoughts of being an actress or a supermodel and settle for appearing in local amateur theatrical productions as a ... dickhead.

## Midday and fourteen and a half minutes

Oops, too late!
   Just tried to get the pumpkin off and discovered that it's stuck, stuck, stuck!
   Oh no, how will I get it off?

## 12.14 and three-quarters of a minute

I've just had an idea.

## 12.14 and nearly sixty seconds

The idea requires a speeding car, a fabulous outfit, an expensive yacht and James Bond.

## Midday and fifteen minutes

I've just realised it's not a very good idea. But I've had another idea and this new idea is much simpler and only requires a tow truck and David Beckham, or a winch and a crane.

## 12.15 *and thirty-two seconds*

Oh, I also don't have either of those. Pity I don't need a 'witch and a pain', then I could have used Miss Priss and Bum Face.

Actually, where are they? Actually, where is *all* of my 'family'? If I try really hard, I can see out of the bottom of the pumpkin and if I turn my head sideways I can look this way and that and I can see that I definitely can't see anyone from my family. This is weird! My cameraman, the floor manager and myself are the only people in the room. Don't tell me God has chosen this precise moment to answer my prayers and has finally sent my family back to the planet that they came from! Wouldn't that be a disaster — the only time in my life that I've ever needed their help and they've gone back to Uranus. Or Their-anus, or whatever!

Of course they might all just be in their own rooms doing their own thing. They might be in the garden, they might be in the bathroom. They might all have decided to have a picnic on the roof! But I can't hear a sound from them or see even a shadow so I suspect my 'family' has left the house altogether and this means that I've won the game which also means that I've won $1 million dollars.

Cooly wooly! I wonder what I'll spend it on. I guess a pumpkin removal operation for a start.

Toodle-e-ooo,

**Midday and seventeen minutes**

Dear Diary,

I've just had a second thought (by this I mean the second thought that I've had on this particular subject, not the second thought that I've ever had in my entire life!!!!!!!!).

Anyway, my second thought was why would my family suddenly not be involved in the game and decide to let me win the million dollars? Particularly when they were the ones who ganged up against me in the first place and wouldn't tell me the rules and kept fining me for silly reasons No, now that I'm thinking more clearly I realise that there is no way in the world that my family would forfeit a million bucks, not when you consider that they tried to sell Grandma to the garbage collector for $2.38.

## Midday and twenty minutes

Okay, so now I'm pretty sure that my 'family' must be here in the house somewhere with their cameramen, probably plotting and scheming to have me eliminated from the show. But enough of them ... back to me and my pumpkin head and my $7.50.

Now, because I don't have a crane and I don't have a winch and I don't have any tools I've decided to just stick my head between my legs, grasp the pumpkin with my knees and then pull my head back as hard and fast as I can.

Here we go!

# One,
## two,
## three.

## Midday and twenty minutes and four seconds

Oh, what a pity. Turns out my head can't reach my knees. Well, never mind. I'll use someone else's. (Someone else's knees, not someone else's head.)

145

Of course I can't use any knees from my family because even if I could find them (my family members, not my knees) they obviously wouldn't help me because they consider themselves to be my opponents and enemies in this game (even though I embrace them all with my new spirit of self-expression and wish for them only that they seek good psychiatric counselling as soon as this ordeal is over).

So this leaves me with no choice but to ask the TV crew to help me, and as I've really only become acquainted with the hairy-legged floor manager, and the guy who had the undies on his camera I guess I'd better start with one of them.

Off the top of my head, or the top of my pumpkin, I think it would probably be wisest to start with the floor manager. I think this for several reasons, all based primarily on the fact that no matter who I choose to seek help from, I can't actually inform the person that I want them to help me because they will no doubt refuse and dob me in and then I'll get fined. I therefore have to simply run full pelt at the chosen person and aim my head between their knees.

So anyway, after much intellectual and arithmetic pontificating the reasons why I'm choosing the Miss Piggy floor manager are:

1/ she's standing closest to me

2/ she won't mistake my run and charge for a sexual advance, and

3/ in her heels she's taller than the cameraman which means that if I were to run towards her my head would reach her knees (whereas if I were to run toward the cameraman my head would only reach his private parts).

So there you go, that is my plan: to run as fast as I can with a pumpkin on my head toward the floor manager's knees.

Wish me luck,

## Midday and twenty-two minutes

One,

Two,

Three,

Chaaaaaaaaaaaaaaaaaaaaaaaaaaaaaaaaaaaaaaaaaa
aaaaaaaaaaaaaaaaaaaaaaaaaaaaaaaaaaaarge!


## Midday and twenty-three and a half minutes

Dear Diary,

Mmmm. That didn't go quite as well as
I'd hoped. In my defence I have to say it is
quite difficult aiming when you have a
pumpkin on your head, and for this reason it
would appear that I completely missed t
floor manager and rammed the cameram
the 'private part area' instead. This is bot      l
and good news.

It is bad news because the cameraman
currently doubled up in pain and rolling
around the floor. It is good news because
spontaneous instinctive reaction when be
assaulted by my pumpkin head was to grab
the pumpkin and hurl it away (unfortunately
with my body still attached). But the pumpkin
did come off my head when I crash-landed on
the ground.

Anyway, the other reason why this is good
news is that there is an upside to the
cameraman's unfortunate incident even
though he has suffered a hideous injury and
we all feel for his pain (not as much, of course,

as he does). Now, I know that this may sound selfish and a little self-obsessed but it's not, so just believe me. Here we go, you see, the fact that the cameraman is rolling around on the floor means that he can't film me which means no-one can see me, so no matter what I do I can't get fined. Which means that I'm free to run out of the room to find Dick Witt, grab him by the tongue and demand that he tell me the rules of the game (once I've released his tongue, of course).

Brilliant,

### Midday and twenty-four and a half minutes

I wonder if I should wear the slippers Mum made for me using two old cushions?

*Midday and twenty-five minutes*
*Running through the house*

Dear Diary,

So here I go. I'm running, running, running through the house. Oh look, there's my family.

I'm running past my two sisters in the hall who appear to have settled very well into the life of intergalactic fame and are looking through the phone book for a celebrity therapist. I'm running past Babette who is in her bedroom going through a plastic surgery catalogue. (If she's really serious about changing her appearance she should be looking though a head replacement catalogue.) I'm running past the Pip who is either trying to impress or depress women across the world by singing a medley of Tom Jones' classics dressed in his shorts/man bra, socks and sandals in the bathroom. I'm running past my mother who is currently knitting her very own TV camera, apparently so that she can 'join in the fun'. And I'm running past my dad who is standing in the kitchen and appears to see his TV show as an opportunity to educate because he is currently giving his cameraman a close-up shot of how to floss your teeth.

No sign of Grandma but no time to stop and look for her. I realise that she may be dead but then again she may be making out with one of the TV crew or, in fact, all of them. Or even just the TV.

*Midday and twenty-six minutes*
*I've just stopped in my tracks*

Dear Diary,
Oh my goodness! I've suddenly realised that if I really want to know what's going on with this show I can just turn on the TV.

Of course I'm positive that if I got busted they would fine me at least $10,000 for turning the TV on, but hey, I can't be blamed for my natural sense of curiosity. I can't help it if I'm like Einstein and Leonardo da Vinci, or a mouse that sticks its head in a trap just to get a bit of stinking cheese.

### *Midday and twenty-six and a half minutes*

Okay, I'm still running, but now my ultimate goal has changed and it's no longer to simply accost Dick Witt, the host and director, and see what he has to say. Oh no, my new goal is to accost Dick Witt, force him to tell me the rules and then run back into the house to watch myself on TV and see if I can get an idea of whether I'm likely to win or not.

### *Midday and twenty-seven minutes*

Okay, I'm still moving like the wind, well a soft summer breeze, well at least a strong fart, but I'm nevertheless running ... all the way out the front door, down the path, across the lawn and over to the driveway and the bus with the satellite dish on top of it.

### *Midday and twenty-seven and a half minutes*

I can hear moaning. Oh no, surely the show can't be that bad! Surely Dick Witt can't be moaning in disappointment? I'd better run into the bus before he does something drastic.

OH NO!

## Midday and twenty-eight minutes
## Gobsmacked in the doorway of the bus

Dear Diary,

I just ran into the bus and found Dick Witt
making out with my grandma! Doesn't he
know that she has a heart condition! Doesn't
he know that she might be dying! Doesn't she
know that this very simple action of hers has
to be the breaking of at least one of the game
rules i.e. no one-hundred-year-old contestant is
allowed to fiddle-de-diddle with the director
in the bus!

But then again, maybe she won't get
punished for breaking the rules. Maybe she'll
be rewarded instead, in particular by someone
in particular, and that someone in particular
(i.e. the host) will make sure that she wins the
million dollars! Maybe Dick Witt as host and
director will want to thank Grandma for her
magnificent performance ... even if it wasn't in
front of the camera.

Honestly, if my grandmother accidentally
wins, just because she's fiddle-de-diddled with
Dick Witt, then I am going to be outraged ...

but I'm also going to be a little impressed and will be asking her for a few helpful grope/make-out tips that I can sell to Lurline when this show is over. (If I'm still talking to Lurline, that is.)

## Midday and twenty-nine minutes

Well this is an interesting situation. I'm standing in a bus that is controlling the TV cameras that are filming my family and broadcasting to the entire world and my grandma is actually in the bus making out with the director and I can't watch.

Neither Grandma nor Dick Witt seems to have noticed me.

I don't know which way to turn and I don't know what's up or down. My grandma, on the other hand, appears to know every move.

Obviously I have to get out of here quick smart because I don't want to get busted. (Though I don't know why I'm the one who's scared of getting busted when they're the ones doing the wrongful act.) But then again, I am supposed to be inside getting filmed and they're both old enough to do what they want. Oh no, that's not right, Grandma is also supposed to be inside getting filmed, and she's way too old to do what she wants even if she is just going to go back inside the house and do her impression of a corpse (which is certainly not what she's doing right now, but is sort of what the director's doing). Actually, why is the director just lying there like that? Is this some new form of romance or has he actually seen me out of the corner of his eye and is just pretending to be dead so that I don't grab his tongue and make him tell me the rules? No, that would be stupid because judging by what he was doing with Grandma only moments ago he seems to like having his extremities grabbed.

Confusederamo,

**Midday and thirty and a half minutes**

Dear Diary,

Oh no, it has suddenly occurred to me that Dick Witt is actually dead.

Oh well done, Grandma. This must be the thirteenth 'boyfriend' that you've managed to

out-live. (And that's so far this year. And it's
only February.)

### Three minutes later

Okay, well this is bad and this is ... bad. I'm
still standing in the doorway of the bus and
I haven't got a clue what to do. I mean, I've
been caught in some quite awkward situations
with my family in my time but never
anything quite like this. Oh sure there was
the time my 'family' and I went to the zoo and
a crocodile mistook the Pip's head for one of
its eggs and casually sat on it. And there was
the time my mother did such a series of
chronic farts at my christening that the
priest thought gunfire had broken out and
hid under a pew. And there was the time
my father was arrested for wearing a
balaclava in a bank (but he wasn't wearing a
balaclava at all, it was just the way he'd done
his hair).

But never have I really been caught in
quite this situation and I don't have a clue
what to do.

Of course, not having a clue what to do
doesn't mean I'm actually going to do
nothing while I wait for something to do.

Oh no sir-eeeeee. I often haven't got a clue what to do, but it doesn't stop me doing stuff. So while I think of what to do, while I don't have a clue, while Grandma seems distracted and Dick Witt looks dead, I'm going to quietly rummage through the piles of paperwork on Dick Witt's desk and see if I can find any clues as to what the rules of this show are and what we're supposed to be doing.

Over and out,

### Nearly 12.33
### Being a spy in the bus

Dear Diary,

Oh, this is great. I feel like some fabulous international super sleuth.

And it's also good that I don't have to worry about Grandma hearing or seeing me because her eyesight is pretty bad and her hearing is dreadful. Well sometimes it's dreadful and sometimes she can see and hear. I guess in summary it all pretty much depends on the mood she's in and how good looking he is, but most of the time she chooses to be a bit like a horny potato with arms and legs.

**12.33 pm**

Okay, I've found quite a few pieces of paper. The first hundred or so seem to be scraps with women's names and phone numbers written on them so I think I'll chuck them in the bin because I'm sure he wouldn't want Grandma to find them. But then again I don't think she'd be threatened by the volume of women's numbers because Grandma's collection of men's phone numbers is pretty well the national phone book.

Other bits of paper have gym appointments and therapy appointments written on them and I've also found a few of Dick Witt's handwritten messages to remember his wife's birthday, his anniversary and the names of his two children.

There's also a note here to remind him to ring his accountant and another one to remind him to buy a yacht. There's a photo of his mother (who looks remarkably like Grandpa) but there's no photo of his wife or kids. A commissioned portrait of his dog is hanging on the wall but there's no sign of any paperwork at all that relates to the show he's meant to be hosting and directing.

How frustrating, how annoying, how inconceivable and unlike any Bond movie. Within two minutes I was supposed to find every piece of information I wanted when I started rifling through these pages and now, the only ones that are left are blank ... Ooooooooooooops!!!!!!!!!!!!!!!

**12.34 pm**

I just bumped a crappy styrofoam cup that was sitting on the desk and now all this algae-coloured cold, old coffee goo is running all over the desk and the papers.

Oh well, I suppose it doesn't matter. I mean he is dead after all and there was nothing of any value to me lying there.

Hey

wait

a

minute!

Now that they're wet, those blank pieces of paper suddenly seem to have writing all over them!

They must have been written in some sort of invisible ink that was triggered to appear when it was dampened. Oh this is fantastic because I think I just found what I was looking for.

The top piece of paper says:

'The goal of our show is to prove that greed will always win. We are pitching members of a family against each other to show that when offered enough money to compete and destroy loved ones, greed will conquer everything ... even the bonds of blood.'

Ah der!

Well I think we all knew that and I don't think that's any big secret that needed to be printed in invisible ink. Maybe there's something else here that I should read.

Oh here's a Swiss bank account number, here's the combination to his safe and here's something very interesting. Oh no, it's not, I think it's his cholesterol level. Never mind, there's one more previously blank page to be read so I'll read that and then get out of here.

'It is unfortunate that we have been forced to use this particular family because they're not at all the sort of people that we wanted. We were hoping for a perfect family, a family with 2.4 children, a dad with a steady job and a mother who loved baking. We at no time wanted stepmothers, stepfathers and aged grandmas. We were hoping for a family with a regular pet like a dog, not a fish finger they keep in the freezer. We wanted a family with a four-wheel drive vehicle who watched television at night and didn't wear clothes that could double as modern sculpture in the Museum of Recycled Crap. In retrospect, was it too much to ask for a simple family who laughed and talked and played cricket together in the backyard? Was it too much to ask for a family that had a living room with real furniture in it as opposed to knitted bits and pieces modelled on things you might find in a fruit bowl! But more than any of this was it too much to ask for a family that quite simply loved each other? With Fleur having been selected as our main focus this show is destined to fail because without love among the family this show has no challenge, no insight and no profundity and all it really boils down to is a group of lazy, selfish people who will do whatever it takes to walk all over each other. It's too obvious. And to be honest we would have achieved exactly the same thing if we'd offered this family a prize of one dollar instead of one million.'

Well that's outrageous, that's offensive, that's hurtful and that's possibly defamatory and I think that I should definitely call a lawyer. It is absolutely not true that anyone in my family would compete against each other on international television for a prize of just one dollar. $1.50 maybe, but not ever for just one dollar.

Oh, I couldn't agree with myself more,

**50 seconds later**

Dear Diary,

Enough of this hanging around reading dead people's private correspondence because there'll be plenty of time to do that with Grandma's mail when she finally pops off. Time is running out and I haven't found the rules yet. Where could they be, where could they be? Should I just spill stuff on everything and see if any magic writing appears, or should I look behind paintings, between fake walls or underneath his dead body to find where the rules are hidden?

Oh, there they are, on a massive white board fastened to the wall. Gee, lucky I noticed them! So what do these rules actually say, there seems to be a million of them.

1. a chosen family will be filmed for seven days and seven nights

2. each family member will be followed 24 hours a day by their own personal cameraman

3. each family member is to wear a battery-pack microphone throughout the duration of the program

4. family members may leave the house but not the premises, and they are never to go anywhere without their microphone and cameraman

5. there will be no obscene gestures made by the family

6. no family member is to attempt to hide from the camera

7. no family member is to attempt to communicate in a manner that cannot be seen or heard by the entire world (by this we don't mean they have to talk really loudly, we just mean they can't cover up their microphones)

8. no family member is allowed to swear (cameramen are of course permitted to swear)

9. no family member may endanger the lives of others (in the pursuit of a better shot cameramen are permitted to)

10. no family member may communicate with anyone other than their family members

11. the breaking of rules will lead to an immediate on-the-spot fine of $10,000. This amount is to be deducted from the million dollar prize should that person win

12. the breaking of more than four rules will lead to expulsion

13. during the course of the seven days the family members will be set a series of challenges

14. the family members will not necessarily be told of the challenges, they will simply find themselves experiencing them

15. each evening the live international TV audience will vote on the way they feel the family members have responded to the challenge. One house member will be eliminated each night

16. family members are actively encouraged to lie, cheat and betray their fellow family members

17. it is considered to be fabulous if the audience vote is swayed by the manipulation

of family members working against each other to win

    18. the final remaining family member will be declared the winner and receive a cheque for the sum of one million dollars

Well, just give me the cheque now babies, because there ain't no-one else winning this batch of cash!!!!!!!!!!!!!!!!!!!!!!!!

*Two seconds later*

Oh, I just saw a P.S. It says:

19. the floor manager is considered to be a member of the family and is allowed to give the family notes

Well. Welcome to the zoo, floor manager.

**12.41 pm**

Yikes, look at the time! I should run back to the house but what about the dead body and my grandma and the spilt coffee? Plus my cameraman will be 'up and at it' soon and I still haven't decided what to do. Actually, that's not quite true because I have decided to do one thing and that's to think all of this out loud so as to give myself the illusion that I'm not alone.

I mean, I'm not alone because Grandma's in here with me, but she's in a sort of post-love trance and doesn't seem to have realised that the director is dead, and presumably she just thinks he's sadly lacking in conversation.

I don't know what to do. I wish I could ring someone or ask someone's advice. (This probably means I must be desperate because the only person I've ever asked for advice was the school counsellor and when I asked her what she thought I should do with the rest of my life she said, 'Fleur, lengthen your uniform.')

Oh what to do, what to do? The director's dead, my grandmother killed him, my home life is being broadcast on international TV, there's a million dollars up for grabs and I've suddenly remembered that now that the pumpkin's been removed from my head I have a glaring zit on my forehead.

I am alone without a clue what to do and yet I know I'm not helpless or about to give up because I come from a long line of Trotters and they don't call us Trotters for nothing. No, they call us Trotters because in times of great stress we do not run away, we do not gallop away, we elegantly trot (and just hope that this surprises our enemies so profoundly that they stare in amazement rather than shoot).

Yet somehow trotting away at a time like this doesn't seem quite right. It seems a little sheepish, a little contrived, a little, shall we say, ridiculous. So what I must do is trottteth-not but rather listen to the messages of my other ancestors, those from my mother's side who were not quite so attention seeking as my father's. I know that somewhere deep inside me, imprinted on my genes, is the stamp of the code of behaviour of these ancestors and all I have to do is listen.

Love,

*12.44 pm*

Dear Diary,

Okay, I just tried to contact my maternal ancestors, but it appears they're not home, and I couldn't leave a message because answering machines hadn't been invented then.


*12.45 pm*

I've decided to just walk out of the bus like nothing happened.

So, my plan now is to get back into the house and resume the position I fell in right after the cameraman hurled the pumpkin off my head. I know I have to hurry to get back in because even if my cameraman were an actor in *Days of Our Lives* where he'd been in a car accident after meeting his long-lost identical twin who was married to his sister who was beautiful and irresistible but had a terminal disease then, even then, someone would have made him conscious by now and he'd be 'up and about'. So, I'm thinking the cameraman is about to recover from 'the massive vegetable in the groin incident' and then he will recommence filming, so before the world realises I'm not in front of the camera I'd better just get in front of the camera and resume my natural lifestyle, with either a bike helmet or a post-it note covering the zit on my forehead.

Gorgeous,

*12.45 and a squidgy bit pm*
*Running up the driveway*

Dear Diary,

Now I'm running up the driveway, over to the footpath, in the front door, past my assorted relatives and back into the living room just by the couch. But I'm not just running, oh no-no-no! I'm also using this travelling time to think about strategy and tactics because all the horrible and untrue things that I read about me and my family in Dick Witt's office have made me determined to really rev myself up to focus on winning that money from him.

If I were a football player I'd be listening to some really motivating theme song right now, something profound and inspiring with lyrics like, 'Yeah, it's a fight, but we'll be right, 'cause tonight's the night we're gonna prove our might.' But unfortunately, the only song I can remember is our family anthem, *We Are The Trotters, Like Little Pig's Feet*.

Ding-a-ling,

**12.47 pm**
**Back in the living room**

Dear Diary,

Okay, well I'm back in the room where it all started and it would appear that absolutely no-one has noticed that I've been absent. This, of course, is yet another sad reflection on either my overall level of charisma or just the impact I have on my family. But the good thing about my family not noticing whether I'm here or there is that I'm able to resume my former position without any hassle whatsoever. So then the only thing I need to do is simply play the game and win the one million dollars and then go shopping for the first pair of high-heeled shoes I've ever owned that Mum hasn't made out of thongs and ice-cream cones.

Yeah to me,

**12.49 pm**

Dear Diary,

Ooooh, this is great. I'm getting back into position. I feel fabulous and ready to naturally play me being natural, conquering all foes and winning *Trotting with the Trotters*. I've left Grandma in the bus to find her own way back to the house. Being a little old and occasionally fuzzy in the head, Grandma is very used to wandering off and having to find her own way home, so I know that she will ultimately get back here ... even if it does take her a year or two.

And the dead director, Dick Witt? Well, I feel very bad about that. Of course I wonder if I should have helped him, I wonder if maybe he really was dead, I wonder if I should have at least anonymously called for an ambulance or a funeral company or a fumigator. But they've told us this is a game where you have to win at all costs and that's exactly what I'm planning on doing. One by one I'm eliminating my foes ... and step by step I'm getting closer to buying my first bra ... and I can't believe I'll actually finally own one that's not made out of egg cups and elastic.

It's about time,

*fleur*

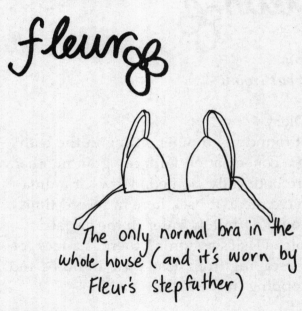

The only normal bra in the whole house (and it's worn by Fleur's stepfather)

**12.50 pm**

Dear Diary,
Oh no, all of a sudden I'm feeling really weird. I think I must be coming down with something because I'm worried about

Grandma. I've never worried or actually cared about anyone else before and I really don't like to feel like this. So I think I might tell my mother all about Grandma so that she can worry about Grandma instead.

Good idea,

**12.52 pm**
**In the bathroom**

Dear Diary,

I just found my mother sitting in the bath having a conversation with my grandmother. (They're both fully clothed.) Wow, Grandma must have made it back here in record time. She should definitely enter in the geriatric Olympics. (That's assuming there is a race for people escaping from dead guys in buses and then hopping in the bath.)

**12.52 and a half pm**

Mum just said she knows all about the dead director in the bus and that's why she went and rescued Grandma.

What! I know mothers are supposed to have eyes in the back of their heads, but surely their eyes can't see through walls, down halls, out front doors, along garden paths, up some stairs and into a bus parked in the driveway!

Wow,

**12.59 pm**

Dear Diary,

Hello, I'm back after doing a bit of research.

See, I had no idea how Mum knew about all this so I asked Mum if she's psychic like me and those aunts that I mentioned earlier and Mum replied that of all the things she might have thought I was about to say, that certainly wasn't one of them. So I guess she isn't psychic.

So then I asked her how she knew that Dick Witt was dead and she proceeded to do the most rebellious thing that I've seen her do since the time I remember watching her put a small bag containing one orange worth of orange peel inside the neighbour's wheely bin about seven years ago. And in fact the act she was doing now was much more rebellious than orange peel because the consequences were potentially so enormous. I mean, sure, when she put the orange peel in the neighbour's wheely bin she risked getting busted and perhaps hosed by the neighbour, but she didn't risk losing $10,000 or perhaps being expelled from a game that could win her one million dollars! And that is precisely what she was doing right now by preparing to break several of the game's rules.

Oh yes, she pulled a shower cap right down over her face so that the television cameras couldn't read her lips and she covered her microphone with her hand and got ready to say something very, very serious. And as I watched her do this two thoughts ran through my mind: the first one was 'SAVE MUM' but the second thought was 'Oh good, now someone else is doing something wrong. Fabulous, she'll get busted and perhaps eliminated from the show and that means less people competing for the prize and a bigger chance for me to win.' Interestingly enough, it was at the precise moment that I'd just finished my second thought when my foot slipped on the wet bathroom floor and I fell on top of Mum, so it looked like I was trying to save her.

So anyway, while I lay on my mother she seized the opportunity to whisper urgently in my ear. But unfortunately I couldn't hear a word of it so I said 'What?' and she mumbled something which I think was 'Don't say what, say pardon,' and so I said 'pardon?' and she repeated her original sentence but I still couldn't understand a word of it and even worse began to see through the shower cap that she was starting to go blue from lack of oxygen. Which is not a safe colour to be even if it is rather flattering to your eyes.

So then I began to use my index finger to tap-tap-tap sort of poke my mother's shoulder. I was of course sending her a message in morse code, but my mother's only reply was to say 'Ouch!' So then I pretended I was about to sneeze, reached over for the toilet paper, pulled on it as though I needed a square to blow my nose on, and then acted like the toilet paper was trying to kill me by wrapping itself around my head. Then, with toilet paper wrapped around my head, disguising my mouth so that no-one could lip-read what I said, I leant over close to my mum, took a very deep breath and said, 'Wigglers.'

Now I realise that of course I didn't need to cover my head with toilet paper to say this single word and in covering my head I was in fact endangering my own chances of surviving in the game, but I guess I just got excited at the thought of actually having a conversation with my mother that wasn't about tidying my room. And I guess I must have also, subconsciously, always wanted an excuse to wrap toilet paper around my head sort of like a low-budget Ninja.

Anyway, the point is that 'wigglers' is our family's very personal earlobe language. It's sort of like morse code but you use your earlobes. I don't mean you use your earlobes to tap-tap-tap a message on your mother's shoulder, I mean you look at someone and you don't seem to be talking, but all the while your earlobes are wiggling and sending very precise messages.

The method works quite effectively and has been honed by generation after generation of usage. Our family first started using wigglers in the early 1500s because everyone in the family had such bad breath that they thought it best not to open their mouths.

*1.37 pm*

My mother hasn't really grasped what I'm
doing, but she doesn't need to because
Grandma's understood and is telling me with
her earlobes that my mum knew that the
director was dead because the floor manager
told her.

The floor manager, eh? Who is this floor
manager? Is it someone on our side, or is it
someone working for the TV company who's
just pretending to be on our side?

And more to the point, how did the floor
manager know that Dick Witt is dead?

Is she a spy?

Is she a perve?

## Is she psychic?

*1.40 pm*

My grandmother just said that the floor
manager knew because everyone in the TV
crew heard me announce it through their
headphones because when I was speaking to
myself in the bus I was still wearing my
microphone.

Oh.

## 1.40 and half a minute pm
## Still in the bathroom

Dear Diary,

Okay, well the two cameramen here in the bathroom with us sure seem pretty relaxed considering that their director has just been murdered by my grandmother. But actually now that I think about it why are there only two cameramen here when there are three family members? Where is my cameraman? Surely he can't still be rolling around on the floor groaning about the pumpkin incident? Honestly, men are so pathetic when it comes to pain there's no way they could handle being a woman. I mean, everyone knows that men couldn't handle childbirth but I reckon they couldn't even handle any of the fundamental agonies that are essential to womanhood — you know, like leg waxing, eyebrow plucking and G-strings.

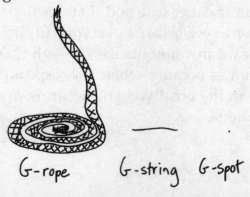

G-rope          G-string   G-spot

But enough of that. We have one cameraman missing and no cameraman is allowed to let his family member out of his sight. Which now that I think about it raises the question as to just how my grandmother managed to get into the bus and kill Dick Witt without being followed by a camera.

I have a sneaking suspicion that my grandmother has either bribed her cameraman with a sum of money to leave her alone or else scared him off by threatening to charge him with sexual harassment (by this I don't mean that she would have threatened to have the police arrest him for sexually harassing her but rather that she would actually charge *at* the cameraman and then sexually harass him).

I guess the third option might be that my grandma is actually in a conspiracy with the organisers of this program. But then why would they want her to go in and kill their director? And besides, I'm sure Grandma wouldn't be a traitor like that. I mean, she may be a manipulative old nymphomaniac but I wouldn't dare want to believe that she's fundamentally a cheat. (Although it would explain where I get it from.)

I think at this point I should ask my mother what she thinks the death of the director means.

**1.42 pm**

My mother just asked if I could give her a clue.
U
n
b
e
l
I
E
V
A
B
L
E.
Love,

**1.42 and three seconds pm**
**Running around**

Dear Diary,
  Well my mother and Grandma are still
sitting in the bath but Mum's decided we need
to call a family meeting to tell everyone about

the host/director's death. Bizarrely enough I agree with her because as far as I can see the TV show is going to have to be cancelled, which means that all of us are effectively going to miss out on one million dollars. Oh sure, the TV channel could try and get another director but he won't have the same vision, the same eye, the same idea and so the whole thing will be an enormous disaster and the show will be a ratings swan dive and a flop and we can't do that to dead Dick Witt because the thought of such a failure would kill him.

So anyway, Mum's made me organise the meeting because she says she doesn't want to get up and do it because she's having much too much of a relaxing time just soaking in the bath (even though there's no water in it). So now I'm running around the house and telling all my 'family' members about the meeting in the bathroom and they've all sort of agreed to come without asking too many questions. (Although Babette did ask if she should bring a plate of food and Miss Priss asked what she should wear and I told her that because the meeting is in the bath she really should come nude.)

Love,

**1.47 pm**

Dear Diary,
  You know it's weird but while I've been
running around I've thought I've caught a
glimpse of something moving out of the
corner of my eye. Everywhere I've gone I've
thought I've seen a shadow lurking behind me.
I really don't know what it is. I don't think it's
the cameraman, so I'm guessing it's the ghost
of the director, Dick Witt.

  Anyway, I'm running back to the bathroom
now ready to meet everyone for the family
meeting. The whole bunch of them is there
including Babette who's brought a plate full of
canned asparagus wrapped in raw bacon, and
Miss Priss who really has arrived nude (and
even though she is obviously the only person
at the bathroom meeting who has no clothes
on, Miss Priss still has that look of superiority

on her face that says, 'Well at least I'm properly dressed for the occasion').

Yep,

**1.49 pm**
**In the bathroom**

Dear Diary,

It's pretty crowded in here because it's not a very big bathroom, and there are seven people who were invited to the meeting and five of them have cameramen with them. Personally, I don't know why this many cameramen have tried to squeeze in because the only shots any of them can possibly get in such tight confines are close-ups of bald spots (from Dad, the Pip, Mum, Babette and Grandma).

Anyway, I've just told everyone about the death of Dick Witt, and now Bum Face and the Pip are both sobbing inconsolably and saying that they'll miss him (even though they only first learnt of his existence about four hours ago and I can't be sure either of them ever actually met him personally).

I'm interrupting their sobbing to raise the question of how we're going to cope as a family when the show is cancelled and we miss out on a million dollars. But now all of a sudden Bum Face has said we don't have to miss out on a million dollars because we can sue Grandma for killing the host and the director. Everyone seems to agree that this is a brilliant idea and I'm sure it is, except for the fact that Grandma doesn't have a cent and I'm pretty positive that she's not insured for accidental death of a middle-aged bloke with a ponytail.

Realising that this isn't a possibility Dad has just said not to worry because he's quite sure that he can direct the show, but I think we're all sure he can't. Especially when you consider that the only thing my dad has ever directed was the first (and last) annual Budgewoi slide show and he was the only entrant and the projector didn't work so we had to get everyone to just pass the individual slides around and people got so bored and frustrated with the whole process that they started a fire on the floor of the scout hall and everyone threw the slides into the fire and then the hall burnt down. Yes, so considering all that I don't think that we should let my father direct the TV show.

Personally, I'm wondering what the cameramen think about all of this. Like, do they think that there's any point in continuing? I mean, this is their job, this is their livelihood, this is their reputation, this is their career!

In fact for all we know maybe the show's already stopped broadcasting! (Well if it has I wish that someone would tell us because then I could stop trying to make myself look really skinny by sucking in my stomach until it's sort of concave.)

But assuming the show hasn't been cancelled yet, we should probably get the cameramen to vote on whether or not we should just cancel the whole thing. But I suppose I should also ask everyone for their vote on whether the cameramen should vote, but damn it, I've been nice and respectful for about four minutes now and I couldn't be bothered overdoing it.

### A moment later

Okay, we're just waiting for all the cameramen to vote.

We're still waiting.

Still waiting.

Still waiting.

My goodness! How long can it take to stick your arm up in the air?

**1.50 pm**

Okay, apparently the problem is that the cameramen can't vote until all the cameramen are here and my cameraman is still missing. There's no sign of him absolutely anywhere although he must be here somewhere because I can hear the director talking to him through the headphones he wears that are turned up way too loud.

# Hey, wait a minute!

# What?

I can hear the director's voice through the headphones!!!!!!!!! But ... but ... is he haunting us ... did he record his voice before he died?
*OR IS HE IN FACT NOT DEAD AT ALL?*

OH MY GOODNESS! COULD THIS BE THE CHALLENGE THAT THEY WEREN'T GOING TO TELL US ABOUT AND WE WERE JUST GOING TO FIND OURSELVES EXPERIENCING!!!!!!!!!!!!!!

Well I guess the first thing I should do is find out if that stupid git is dead or not. And if he isn't then I should probably stop referring to him out loud as 'that stupid git'.

There's only one way to find out for sure if he's dead, and that's to run back to the bus in the driveway and poke him with a stick.

Oh yes, I know what you're thinking — wouldn't it be easier to just see if he's breathing or perhaps has a pulse or is even lying there getting eaten by maggots. But no, experience with my grandmother has taught me that all these things can be faked and that the only sure-fire way to tell if someone or something is dead is to poke them with a stick.

That's what we do with Grandma, and that's what we do with small marsupials that Dad has run over on the road.

**1.52 pm**

Dear Diary,

Okay, I've just used wigglers to tell my 'family' that I'm going to run to the bus in the driveway to see if the director is dead, but I think some family members may not have quite the grasp of the language that I'd hoped because the Pip, Miss Priss, Bum Face and Dad all just asked if they could 'have fries with that'.

Of course with so many people not understanding what I said it may be that *I* don't have quite the grasp of earlobe language that I thought I did ... but I doubt it. And besides, Grandma has asked if she can come to the bus too (which is just absolutely gross because I know that the only reason she wants to see if Dick is alive is so that she can do it with him again.) And also, the other thing I have to keep in mind and be very cautious of is that Grandma is more than likely working for the other side and is basically my enemy.

Please Note: I don't feel very comfortable at the thought that my grandma is my enemy but then again, I don't feel very comfortable about the fact that all these people are allegedly my relatives so I guess I should just deal with it.

*1.53 pm*

# STOP

# Yes,

# STOP

I've decided that I can't deal with it.
In fact, I've decided that I can't deal with
any of it.

I mean, even if I'm right and this entire
'family' is a group of aliens who
accidentally landed on this planet and are
simply passing their time until a sudden
change of wind transforms them into the
single-celled insecty things that they once
were and then blows them back to their
planet of origin they are still my family,
and at the moment this grandma is the only
grandma I've got. And yes, she may be old
and she may be a nymphomaniac and she
may occasionally smell like some sort of
bizarre combination of mothballs, talcum
powder and compost, but if I call her
Grandma then she's my grandma and for the
moment I couldn't bare the thought of her
betraying me to win a prize in some TV
competition. (Although if she did win one
million dollars she might buy me a better
birthday present this year. Actually, if she dug
a worm up out of the backyard and gave it to
me it would be better than last year's birthday
present, which as I recall was the crust from
her toast.)

Anyway, enough of this thinking business.
There really is only one way to determine if

my grandmother is working for the enemy
and that is to ask her.

So on we go,

**1.54 pm**
*In the bath with Grandma*

Dear Diary,

I just asked Grandma if she's working for the
enemy and she said no. Well actually, the first
time I asked her she said yes but I ignored this
because I'm pretty sure she only said it to
impress the floor manager with how exotic
and risk-taking she is.

(Personally, I don't know why she thinks she
needs to say this sort of thing to sound like a
risk-taker, she could just confess to the fact
that even though she's one thousand and five,
she wears a G-sting and no bra.)

Anyway, the point is that after saying
yes she then said no. So now Grandma can
come out to the bus with me because as I
said, when I asked if she was working for
the enemy her answer was in the negative
and that's all the proof I need (unless she

thought I asked her, 'Do you want an enema?').

And besides, dear Diary, even if she is working for the enemy that doesn't mean I can't be on her side too. I mean, this game is all about winning the money, no matter what that involves — betrayal, lies, deception, manipulation ... nothing more really than it takes to get someone to do your homework for you and hand it in on time.

### 1.55 and a bit pm

Just between you and me, dear Dairy, I think that Grandma is innocent.

### 1.56 pm

# Oh, I don't believe it!

We've been interrupted and stopped!
The floor manager just handed me a note that said I have to think my thoughts out loud.
So I just said out loud, 'I can't believe the floor manager just told me that I have to think my thoughts out loud.'
Brilliant,

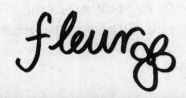

## 1.56 and three-quarters pm

Dear Diary,

The floor manager has just handed me another note. I'm beginning to think she's a bit keen on me. I hope the message doesn't say 'I love you'. Or even worse, 'I WUV U'.

## 1.57 pm

Oh no. I mean, oh yes. The note isn't about love. It's about another new rule! Apparently a new rule's been invented and it's now a punishable offence to think to yourself and you have to actually say everything that you're thinking out really loud.

## 1.58 pm

Well I think that sucks. As if we're not under enough stress trying to look slim, attractive and nice and kind without being obligated to share our private thoughts as well. Can you imagine the pressure I'm now feeling about what I'm thinking — you know, is my thought interesting enough, is it funny, is it profound, is it pathetic, is it racist, is it elitist, is it dumb, is it vain, is it flippant, is it stolen from Enid Blyton, will my thought bring peace to the world, how's that zit going on my forehead?

Oh damn it, I've decided not to think at all. Not thinking seems to be so much easier. It's what everyone else in my family does and it appears to work just fine for them.

Great, I'll be thoughtless.

**2.01 pm**

Dear Diary,

Yes, I am currently not thinking a single thing except that now I know exactly what it must be like to be Miss Priss and Bum Face.

**2.01 and a quarter pm**

So that no-one can tell that I'm thinking and not saying my thoughts out loud, I'm trying to have a blank face like a snooker ball.

### 2.01 *and a half pm*

I suppose if I were really competitive and wanted to make everyone look bad then I should have thought that thought about Miss Priss and Bum Face out loud.

In fact as I'm standing here looking like a snooker ball not letting myself think, I'm actually having quite a few thoughts. My first thought is that if Grandma is working for the enemy then maybe some of my other family members are also working for the enemy. My second thought is that maybe everyone else is working for the enemy and I'm the only one who isn't. My third thought is that maybe I'm the enemy. And my fourth thought is that I liked it so much better when I was allowed to think as much as I wanted and coincidentally didn't think much at all.

Now I don't know who to trust but I guess I have the choice of either trusting everyone or no-one.

It's so cosmic,

## 2.01 *and a half plus a bit pm*

Dear Diary,
   I've decided not to trust anyone but to act
like I'm trusting everyone.


## 2.02 *pm*

I've just made an announcement that
for anyone who's wondering what I'm
thinking I'm thinking about how much
I love my family and all the people working
on this show.


## 2.02 *and twelve seconds pm*

I can tell that none of them trusts me.
   But enough of what these people think.
They're only my family and my workmates.
What about the rest of the world? They're the
ones who'll be voting for the winner. Oh yes,
those billions of complete strangers are much
more important than anyone else. They
represent money and success so I must find
out what they think of me.
   Of course I guess I could wait until the
voting tonight, but that might be too late, and

if I can get some idea of how I'm being portrayed then maybe I can change my image to make me more popular (you know, the same way Madonna does).

So the first thing I have to do is get to a television and see just exactly how I'm looking.

Brilliant once again,

**2.04 pm**

Dear Diary,

I'm wandering back through the house to the living room near where the pumpkin came off my head. Gee, I hope that the scene with me hurling my pumpkinhead at the cameraman's groin never actually made it onto television because then all the really scared people of this world, like my family, will have vegetables banned from their households on the grounds that they can be used as dangerous weapons. On the other hand, they might try to ban my head ... which, for entirely different reasons, is the same thing I tried to do to Babette. Or they might just try to ban men's groins (which is something my mother and her friends have been trying to do for absolutely years).

**2.05 pm**

Okay, I'm over in the other corner of the living room now and I can see that the TV has been stolen.

What

a

disaster,

fleur

## 2.06 and a half pm

Dear Diary,

Okay, I've just run back into the bathroom and told Dad that our TV has been stolen and he's told me that we never owned one.

Never owned one? Who is he kidding? We haven't been allowed to watch any TV for the past eleven years but I'm sure we did actually have one because I can remember we used it as a snack table at Christmas time when I was little and put all the bowls of Mum's homemade canned pineapple and smoked oyster pikelets on it. I also remember that some sort of weird toxic combination of ingredients dissolved the plates immediately and then dissolved the TV.

AHA! Now I remember where the TV went. It dissolved and the molten plastic was bought by the government as part of their MOBILE INCORRECT USE OF FOOD INGREDIENTS EXHIBITION. Oh and I also remember that I suggested they take the Pip as well. But they said they couldn't because he 'wasn't any use'. And I said that's precisely my point.

**2.07 pm**

But wait a minute. If we don't have a TV what were we watching last year when the Queen gave her annual Christmas address?

Actually, now that I think about it I'm pretty sure it was just a melon in a bonnet. And now that I think about it again I'm pretty sure I commented at the time that it's the most attractive and alive that I've seen the Queen look in years.

Okay, well that's that then,

**2.09 pm**
*In the kitchen*

Dear Diary,

Anyway, I'm in the kitchen now trying to build a TV using the microwave and a hair curling wand. It was really hard to find the right equipment to use and even more difficult to find a spare powerpoint. As you can imagine there are extension cords and double adaptors absolutely all over the place and a whole bunch of technical guys are trying to make sure that this massive TV set-up with its cameras, microphones and satellites doesn't overload the power system and make it all explode. I wish they were here all the time, then I'd feel safer whenever Dad tries to set off a rocket launch using his electric toothbrush at the same time as Mum's shaving her legs with the lawnmower.

But then again, maybe I don't really need a safety backup. I mean, there's no reason at all to think that I wouldn't be able to cope if there was an electrical drama in our house. Oh sure, I have no experience, no qualifications and a pretty nonexistent interest level but hey, that's never stopped me doing anything before. Actually, that's never stopped me doing *everything* before.

Actually, that's not fair on myself. I am a very positive, enthusiastic, optimistic person, but I don't like to show it because I can't see the point.

Well I can see the point, but then I can't see the point, because to be perfectly frank there is no point. So the point I can see is no point at all. That's right, because to be honest there is no point in being Madam Sunshine-Hope-and-Joy in a house where happiness is pretty well looked at as some sort of sign of the devil.

I can remember as a baby whenever I tried to smile my mum would just assume I had wind. This response continued until I was about eleven when I finally got so tired of being thrown over my mother's knee and having my back patted every time I smiled that on my twelfth birthday I made a resolution to never smile again.

That day was actually a massive turning point in my life because once I stopped smiling my family began to treat me differently. All of a sudden my family welcomed me into their arms. Suddenly I wasn't different and scary, suddenly they embraced me as one of their own and they became, well ... sort of like a family. But the weird thing was that the more comfortable they became with me, the less comfortable I became with them because I wasn't happy with the new non-happy me. I longed to be my former smiling self and I soon realised that I couldn't just give up cold turkey.

So I tried to cut back on my smiles, maybe only have one after lunch and then two after dinner but soon I became ashamed of myself. I wasn't happy having to sneak off to the bathroom for a quiet smile, or having to dash behind the shed for a quick happy face. I wanted to be open and honest.

Ah yes, thinking about me all that time ago having just turned twelve, I'm astounded at my strength of character. I can't believe the driven, focused, proud girl that I was. I find it difficult to reconcile her with the glum bum who sits here now, writing a diary while she tries valiantly to make a television out of two implements which, even if I were a massive technological genius, would still only really combine to create curly french fries.

You know, dear Diary, I look at the former strong-willed me and I long for her sense of purpose and profound self-belief. I look upon her as though she were my hero. And the weird thing is that her is me.

So what happened to that girl so full of promise. Well, she got tired of the lifestyle, the loneliness and the price of being herself. She chose to follow the pack into Glumland and live the life of least resistance. Each day her will to smile grew weaker until one day her grandma told her that people who smile end up with much worse wrinkles than people who never make a facial expression, and with that the girl closed her mouth for good and permanently untwinkled her eyes. Then pretty soon after that my smiling muscles became untoned and I actually couldn't raise a smile. That's right, if I were at school and they wanted us to smile for the school photo the teacher would actually have to use lipstick to draw a smile on my face, and in fact one year I had to hold an upward-bending cocktail frankfurt between my teeth just to make it look like a grin.

### 2.12 pm

Ooooh I just smiled! But that's only because I accidentally sent an electric current up my finger and throughout my entire body, so it was more of an electrical reaction than a spontaneous indication of joy.

I hope the camera didn't catch me looking happy because it will ruin the angle I'm working on i.e. to win the audience's love. (Please Note: I've decided to go for the lonely, pathetic, I need help kind of angle ... the same way that guys do when they're trying to pick up girls.)

I think I'll do a dance of joy, I mean misery. Vote me the winner,

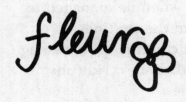

## 2.12 and a half pm

Dear Diary,
   Oh, I've just noticed my cameraman in the doorway. I wonder how long he's been back on board and how long he's been standing there filming me.
   He doesn't look happy to be back at work but he does look sort of relaxed because he's standing there with his legs crossed.

## 2.12 and three-quarters and a half pm

He's coming a little bit closer toward me but his body language doesn't look quite so relaxed now because he's trying to walk with his legs crossed.

## 2.13 pm

Actually, he's not walking at all ... he's sort of twist-drag-hopping and he looks just like the gardener did that time when he managed to successfully escape from the confines of Grandma's clutches but couldn't quite manage to undo the handcuffs that she'd skilfully fastened round his ankles.

Oh yes, the cameraman does look exactly like the gardener and in fact the only difference that I can see between the two men is that the gardener was wearing a swimming costume and Superman cape and the cameraman is not only fully clothed but is also wearing jeans and a T-shirt and one of those private parts protection boxes over his private parts (as opposed to the Pip who used to wear one as a hat ... which is of course further proof that he is a dickhead).

Oh and the cameraman also appears to be waving a handkerchief. Why? Has he just hurled a whopper gob into the air and is now trying to catch it?


## 2.13 and a half pm

Oh no, no gob. Seems he's just waving the piece of white fabric because he's making the inter-national sign of surrender. Gee, I haven't seen anyone do that since a tantrum I threw when I was three and my parents came in begging for me to stop. I remember them waving a pair of white Y-fronts (and the really weird thing was that the Y-fronts were my mum's).

But why would the cameraman want to surrender? Maybe I'm just too ugly and he can't bare to film me anymore. Maybe I'm just too boring. Maybe I'm just too gross and am making him feel ill. Oh my goodness, I feel guilty now! I want to befriend him. I want to say, 'I'll try to be more attractive and not so dull. Please put the hanky and the jockstrap away.'

But instead of giving me a chance to say all of this the cameraman is hopping closer and closer. In the hand that's not holding the white thing I can see some

# CASH!!!

*2.13 and three-quarters pm*

Dear Diary,

Oh, I don't know what happened. Something took over me and I just reached out and grabbed the money and it fell on the ground, so I roughly counted it before I gave it back. And the total was about $10,000. I wonder if this is a trick scenario and if I take the money he's offering I will then actually lose another $10,000, which will mean that on the first day of this game I will have lost $40,000.

I guess I should probably refuse to accept it, just in case it's a trap. In fact, I think that I might really trick the director and tell the cameraman to split the cash into seven equal parts and give it to my family. (I know that sounds like I'm being really nice but actually I'll just take the money back from my family when our lives are no longer being televised.)

HA HA! Yes, that's what I'll do and that'll show that tricky director a tricky thing or two ... assuming that he's alive.

Bravo to me yet again,

**2.14 pm**

The cameraman is still coming toward me, and I can see that he's now not only offering me the money but also thrusting the white thing at me (the handkerchief, not the jockstrap).

### 2.14 and a half pm

Turns out the white thing is a used hanky (gross) with something written on it.

I tell you, if it's written in snot then I'm going to throw up.

### 2.14 and three-quarters pm

Nope, it's written in ink (and I just hope that it didn't come out of his nose).

### 2.15 pm

The note says:

## 'I vote to continue with the show.'

# What!!!!!!!!!!!!!!!!

He votes to continue with the show!!!
Talk about incredibly bad dramatic timing! That whole thing about getting the cameramen voting on whether we all go on with the show was absolutely pages and pages

ago. And, Mr Cameraman, it was also before we realised that the director still appears to be alive and talking to you through your headphones. We've moved on, Mr Cameraman, and we're now dealing with the fact that you are offering me a wad of cash and I'm going through an emotional growth spurt. If this were a movie, mooshy music would be playing. If this were a movie there would be no conversation at this point, just lots of bright and happy pictures of me getting on with being a good and kind person while I worked together with my family and finally found true happiness.

(Actually, if this were a movie probably neither of us would be in it, because we're not good looking enough!)

So there,

Dear Diary,
Oh my gosh, I just took a closer look at the cameraman and realised he's only about

eighteen. No wonder he's been acting like a child because eighteen in male years is about the same age as being five years old for females!

So anyway, what is this cameraman thinking? He's acting like he's been hit in the head, not hit in the groin where he was actually ambushed. Unless the pumpkin-butt in the groin has given him brain damage.

But then again, maybe he isn't that dumb and is simply trying to manipulate me. Maybe he's really smart and just acting dumb. (Mind you, I've credited lots of guys with being really smart and just acting dumb ... and then time proved they were honestly really just dumb. Oh yes, the strong silent intellectual type who is actually just stupid.)

So the dilemma here is to know whether this cameraman is smart, dumb, honest or manipulative. It's such a difficult thing to determine. Do I judge him on his voice, his eyes, or the way his mouth twitches when he talks?

I know, I'll judge him by the most reliable, confronting, straight-shooting way that women know. Oh yes, I will judge him by the method that females have judged males since time immemorial. I will judge him by the only true

indicator of a man's spirit and soul. I will
judge him by his shoes.

I'm a genius,

*2.17 pm*

Dear Diary,

Oh, this is brilliant. Within moments I'll
know whose side he's on. Is he wearing ug
boots, thongs, Cuban-heeled boots, deck shoes
or runners?

*2.17 and a half pm*

He's wearing ski boots! Yes, they look like ski
boots. So what does that mean? Maybe the guy
has really, really cold feet.

Whatever he is, he isn't manipulative
because no-one could try and bend someone
else's mind by wearing that clunky get-up on
the ends of their legs.

But then on the other hand, maybe he's seen
what I'm wearing and thought that I'd find his

look attractive. Doesn't he realise this isn't actually 'my look'? Doesn't he realise that I have no choice, my mother made this for me? This isn't an outfit, this is a uniform! Yes, I'm wearing my prison uniform.

Maybe he wants to help set me free by skiing me away. Good idea! Except there's no snow. And by the look of it there are also no skis.

Okay, well obviously he wants to give me the cash for some reason that I can't possibly imagine so I think I'll take his offer quite seriously. So long as I don't have to actually kill and eat any of my siblings (because you can imagine how revolting they'd taste), then I'm quite willing to do whatever it takes. He might want me to reveal embarrassing facts about my family. He might want me to betray them, or lie about them, or convince them to do things that they might not ordinarily do (you know, like wash daily or remove the green stuff from between their teeth after each meal). Well whatever it is, I'm willing to give it a go.

Maybe he just wants to give me the $10,000 because he likes me. Maybe he's the son of someone really, really wealthy and he's inherited a fortune and he just thought I could do with some of the loose change in his pockets. Maybe his dad is some oil billionaire. Maybe his dad is a drug runner. Maybe the cameraman himself is a drug runner. Maybe the cameraman wants me to do some illegal drug-trafficking thing for him. But then what job could I possibly do for him that would be worth $10,000 with cameras watching my every move? I mean, I doubt he wants me to transport masses of illegal substances from the kitchen to the living room.

But then again, maybe the cameraman has quite simple and kind motives in offering me the money. Maybe the cameraman does freelance work for St Vincent de Paul and they've chosen me as one of their charity cases. I mean, to be honest I probably am willing to sell my soul to him but maybe his motives are entirely innocent.

And then maybe they're not. I mean, what does he get in exchange for giving me $10,000? What does *he* get from this transaction? Does he get promoted, does he get a new pair of shoes, does he get to marry me and take me away to the Himalayas where I shall be a poor but honest princess? (Actually, I won't be that poor because I'll have my $10,000.)

So, maybe he does want to marry me. But why does he want to marry me? Does he love me? How does he know that he loves me?

Is my aura really that magnetic? I doubt it, because the only thing I regularly seem to attract is little bits of fluff in my navel.

So maybe he doesn't want to marry me after all.

But I wonder why the cameraman is giving *me* the $10,000. I wonder why he hasn't offered it to anyone else in my family. But then maybe he has offered the money to everyone else in my family and they all refused!!!!!!!!!!!!!!!!!!!!!!!!

Oh my goodliness. Imagine that!!!!!!

Maybe they refused to take the money because they're stupid. Maybe they refused to take it because they're smart. Maybe they refused because they didn't want to cheat. Maybe they refused because they're good and kind and honest people!

Imagine if my opponents in this game are good and kind and honest people! What a disaster! How the hell can I win against that sort of force! I mean, I can walk all over my family with my devious plots and cunning, clever contrivances but how bad am I going to look if they're all being good. I'm going to look like King Kong treading on a butterfly, I'm going to look like a shark eating a goldfish, I'm going to look like a badly dressed teenage girl who is willing to do whatever it takes to win a million dollars.

Oh, this is a disaster. When did my family get so smart that they worked out this gentle tactic? It's barbaric and cruel and absolutely outrageous and the only thing I can say in reply is,

# 'WHY DIDN'T I THINK OF IT FIRST?'

This is such a clever idea that no-one in my family can possibly have thought of it. One of them must have read about goodness and kindness somewhere. But none of them really reads very much so how does that work? Maybe there was a picture of someone being good and kind that you could colour in on the side of a cereal box. Maybe the whole world is moving toward being good and kind. Maybe goodness and kindness are the new trends! Boy, am I old-fashioned then.

Maybe this show is actually about proving who can be the best person, who has the best heart, who is the kindest and most generous of us all. Maybe the winner isn't the most dastardly one who manages to only look after themselves. Maybe the winner of this game, as judged by the intergalactic audience, is the person who respects others and treats others well. Maybe that's the way the whole of life works. Maybe that's what Jesus and Buddha and Allah believed. Maybe that's what all the world religions are essentially about. Maybe they're not about dominating others but about respecting others and respecting yourself. Maybe they're about peace and genuine harmony, as opposed to the life I've been leading which I guess revolves around being selfish and self-obsessed and believing that the whole world would be a much better place if it actually revolved around me.

But then maybe I don't need to study religions or even think about them. After all, it's a bit hard to take religions seriously when so many of the men involved appear to wear frocks. But you know, the more I think about life itself the more I think I'm right in believing that I've been profoundly wrong ... yep, wrong for my entire life.

It's extraordinary really. Somehow or other, only moments after I was born I began to want to prove something. What, I don't know. Just something. Perhaps that I was better than others, or perhaps that they were just not as good as me. But who was I, what was I, what was my goal in not respecting the fact that everyone I encountered was just as valid as me? (Well maybe not everyone, but I think you get my drift.)

And you know, in my new generous spirit of compassion and consideration of others, I would like to point out that it's not just me in this world who's been selfishly motivated. Heaps of people have the wrong attitude to life, heaps of people seem to think that the purpose of life is to be better than everyone else. You know — richer, prettier, skinnier. But why? What's the point? When you die it's not like anyone's going to write on your headstone:

*Here lies Verity Snot*
*We shall remember her forever*
*(not because she said or did anything incredible,*
*but because she had a very flat stomach)*

Or

*Here Lies Bertrand Le Wedgie*
*He was the richest person in the world*
*(but he still died anyway)*

I guess it all boils down to what you think life is about and why you think we're alive in the first place. I guess it also boils down to where you think you go when you die. Some people think that you just die and get eaten by worms, some people think you are reincarnated and possibly come back to earth as a worm, and some people think you go to heaven to live happily ever after.

I used to think that you just live, do whatever you want, die, and then have someone else clean up after you. But I'm willing to change my entire belief system in order to play this game. I am willing to be kind, generous, magnanimous and other big words for at least the next six days.

Yes, it's the new me,

*fleur*

Old Me    New Me

### 2.18 and three-quarters pm

Excuse me, dear Diary, I just had to go and stand on my cameraman's foot. He was staring at me and holding out the money, but he was nodding off at the same time. Maybe looking at me makes him fall unconscious. Maybe looking at me makes him fall asleep, or even worse, fall into a coma. Maybe I should just hurry up and tell him whether or not I want the money. But I can't hurry up, not when I'm under pressure. It's like when you really need to go to the toilet, and you get in the cubicle and someone yells 'Hurry up!' And suddenly not a droplet drips out.

### 2.19 pm

Oh no, now I need to go to the toilet again. But the bathroom's full of people and there's no way I'm ever peeing in the wild again (even if I was on *Survivor* and stuck on some primitive island for three months).

So yes, anyway, back to me. The truth is I only became spiritual about two minutes ago, but even in the last four minutes I've changed and grown as a human being. I mean, when I first became spiritual I thought it might be a good bludgy way to win this competition, but now I've evolved and become really spiritual in a higher, purer way. That's right. I'm sort of becoming saintly. I think I'm becoming a chosen one. I wouldn't be surprised if I was glowing right now ... or at least wearing some sort of halo.

(Note to self: I wonder if I'd look good in a halo. I wonder if you can choose your halo from a range of different colours so that you can match it really well to suit your lip gloss.)

**2.20 pm**

Okay, so maybe that last thought, the bit about choosing a halo in different colours, didn't quite prove that I've become deeper and more profound. But if you compare it to all the other things I've written in this diary I think that the mere fact I noticed that what I wrote wasn't profound, proves that I have become more profound.

And now I guess the best way to show the world how much I've changed and how fabulous I am is to quietly go out and prove it. But how do I do that? I mean, it's not like there are any homeless people here who I can offer shelter to, and it's not like there are any hungry people here who I can feed, and it's not like there are any needy people who I can just sort of randomly give acts of kindness to (well actually, my entire family is probably needy, but other than all of them there is definitely no-one.)

I guess I should do what all other great spiritual people have done throughout history. I think I should pray for guidance. (My stepfather reckons he does this every week in church, but I'm pretty sure that the real reason why he gets down on his knees so quickly every five minutes is to get a brief peek up the old ladies' skirts.)

Wish me luck with my prayers,

**2.22** *and a half pm*

Dear Diary,

Okay, the spirits didn't answer so I tossed a coin and it came up heads which means ... well I don't know what it means ... but anyway, I told the cameraman, well actually no I didn't tell the cameraman, I told the camera lens, 'Thank you but I cannot accept your ten thousand dollars.'

**2.22 *and three-quarters pm***

The cameraman just said, 'What ten thousand dollars?'

**2.23 *pm***

Oh, turns out he was offering me $10 and I just confused my zeroes, and the only reason he was offering it to me was to stop me charging him in the groin with a pumpkin on my head. Well, after that long drawn-out exchange, it's going to cost you a lot more than that, Mr Cameraman.

Toodle-de-doo,

**2.23 *and a little bit pm***

The camerman heard me think out loud and just collapsed again.

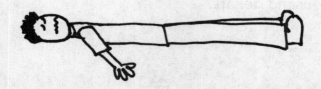

## 2.23 *and two little bits pm*

Okay, well it looks like little old new and improved me is just going to go back to my original plan which was to see how I was being portrayed on TV. Luckily, while I've been writing I've managed to make a television using the microwave and the mix master. The picture's a bit fuzzy, and you have to run around in a circle to watch it, but you can still get the idea of what's going on.

## 2.24 *pm*

I'm very dizzy at the moment, but I know I'm on the right channel because they've just announced that there will be no elimination tonight.

NO ELIMINATION TONIGHT! What does this mean?

Gee, I wonder if that's because we're all so interesting that the television viewers don't want to choose between us. Boy, I hope that's not why, because that would be a very sad reflection on our audience if they found everyone else in my family as interesting as me. I mean, that's like comparing a tornado to drying paint. That's like comparing a newly born baby to a sock. That's like comparing me to seven people who could easily be mistaken for papier-mache bowling pins. What is our audience thinking? What are they watching? How is this program being edited? Why is there no elimination tonight!!!!!

I think I'll say that thought out loud and see if I can get some sort of response from our audience.

**2.40 and a smidge pm**

Okay, well it turns out that there is no audience and that's why there's no elimination tonight. Yes, that's right.

# There is no audience!!!!

**2.40 and five smidges pm**

The floor manager just came up and handed me a note, presumably from the 'dead' director, Dick Witt, and it says:

'You are the most boring family in the world. No-one is watching **Trotting with the Trotters**. This show will no longer be running for seven days but for just 24 hours instead. There will be one audience vote only and it will determine the outright winner.

P.S. If I had my way you'd all be eliminated, because none of you is a winner and you're all losers.'

Well, of course I'm wondering if this is to be taken seriously, because this could be another so-called *challenge* just to throw us off our tracks. I mean, it could very well be that Dick Witt thinks this news will somehow seduce us into relaxing and therefore encourage us to let down our guard. It would be a low-down deceptive manipulative trick ... but that's what I'd do if I were the host/director. (No, actually, if I were the director the first thing I'd do is cut off my stupid grey ponytail.)

But whether this news is another tricky challenge or not it does make me wonder if my family really has been too focused on trying to be too well behaved just because we're on international television. I mean, it is possible that we have been a bit boring. Well, actually that's a stupid thing to say. Because what I mean is that of course it is possible for them to be boring ... because we all know they're always boring. But it is normally completely *impossible* for me to be boring. And now that I think about it, this is the reason why I know that this must be a tricky challenge. In fact, this must be the reason why I'm the one who's been given the note (unless, of course, Miss Piggy has realised that I'm more than likely to be the only one here who can actually read).

Yes, I can see it all now. I have been given the note because I'm being too fabulous and am obviously the audience's most popular family member and therefore am so clearly going to win that the director has tried to cramp my style a bit with this little trick. Obviously he wants me to slow down a bit, to stop being so fascinating, so charismatic, so delightful, so charming, so winnerish! He wants me to let down my guard and give my other family members a chance to be in the running to win. Well let me tell you here and now that there is no chance of that one, Mr Director. I'm in the lead and I'm staying that way. I'm going to spend the next six and a half days being so unbelievably fascinating and magnificent that no-one in their right mind would ever vote me off this show and I will therefore be the winner.

Yeah,

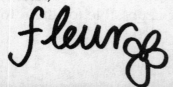

*2.44 pm*

Dear Diary,

My cameraman is crying. Why?

Oh, turns out he's just been told that the show will no longer be broadcasting for a whole seven days, and he will be out of a job from 9 am tomorrow.

Ooooooooooooooooooooooooooooooooooooooo oooooops! Maybe I am really boring.

### Sometime absolutely ages later

Okay, it's about 10 pm. I feel really sad. I'm having a foodless picnic with my family. We were going to go in the roof to have our picnic but we couldn't fit everyone plus their cameramen so we decided to go *on* the roof instead. The view from the roof is actually why my parents bought this home in the first place, because if you built a 210-storey skyscraper here you could have a view of really nice houses.

Anyway, we're on the roof so I'll tell you what happened.

You see a few hours ago I went into the bathroom to explain to everyone that we were being axed because we're not interesting enough and I found them all fighting about whose turn it was to get in the bath. This was pretty embarrassing, dear Diary, because you may remember there was no water in the bath so there was absolutely no reason why anyone would want to sit in it (unless they thought it was some new fun-park ride or something). Honestly, anyone would think that they'd never been in the bath before ... (Actually, now that I think about it ...)

Anyway, they were also fighting about who was more likely to win the money and what they'd do with it if they won. My mother said that she'd give it to the dog home (I wonder if that means us). My father said he'd buy a new electronic nasal hair remover and the Pip said that he'd spend nearly all of it on toilet paper and maybe a new house to keep it all in. Miss Priss said that she'd buy a shop that sells bulletproof underwear and Grandma said that she'd spend it all on winning the heart of Prince Harry (although I'm pretty sure that it's not his heart that she actually wants). Then in a weird twist Bum Face said that she'd give it all to Mum, so then Mum said that she'd give it all to Dad, so then Dad said that he'd give it all to Grandma and then Grandma said, 'Why thank you very much.' And then Babette said that she'd share it equally amongst all those she loved so then everyone started fighting about who would get the 'biggest equal part', not realising that what Babette actually meant by saying she would 'share it equally amongst all those she loved' is that she would keep it all for herself.

I guess it was strange to watch all this and realise that winning the prize money won't make a single bit of difference to my family. Well, I mean it seems that they might fight a bit more, but it certainly wouldn't make a positive difference. So this realisation raised the question, why are we continuing to play this game, why are we willing to sit here until tomorrow morning when the best one of us is chosen by everyone, or no-one, depending on whether or not people tune in now that they know we're being axed. And when they choose which one of us is the best, the question still remains, the best what? That is really the question. I mean, none of us has shown that we're the best anything really and tomorrow all most of us will get the chance to do is prove that we're the best loser. And you know what they say about 'good losers' — 'Show me a good loser and I'll show you a real loser.'

Anyway, after finding my family fighting in the bath I needed a second to think.

Then I needed a couple more seconds to think.

And then a little longer.

And then I couldn't think any more and decided that we had two courses of action here. One was to remain playing the game on the TV show and then end up with one winner and seven losers, and the other was to quit the game and either end up all winners (because of our newly found solidarity and independence) or all losers (because the entire world would be watching us and saying, 'I can't believe they forfeited one million dollars so that they could maintain their pride and regain their lives and do things like spend Saturday nights standing round a barbecue watching their father cook hand-knitted sausages while wearing an apron with plastic bosoms on it.').

So anyway, I couldn't decide which course of action to take so I decided that I should ask my family what they all thought we should do.

Why not? After all, we are all human beings, we all have hearts and minds and pride and instinct, and I thought that together we could decide what was the most intelligent and constructive course of action for us all to take. And that's when the Pip's hunger pains screeched like fingernails down a blackboard and for no associated reason Mum said, 'Hey, let's all go have a foodless picnic on the roof.'

I guess that really what we're having up here is a family meeting and much to my surprise this is actually a pretty good place for it (probably because it's really, really dark and we can't see each other's spooky faces). But even though it's dark up here it's not like we can hide from the filming because all the cameramen are up here with us, including mine, who is now padded up and protected like a footballer. It's night-time so the pictures they're getting must be almost pitch black (except for when they're filming Grandma perving at the assorted cameramen and the glint of her eye lights up the white of her dentures). But anyway, we're all still wearing our microphones so the whole world can hear every word we say (that is, if anyone in the whole world was actually bothering to tune into our television show).

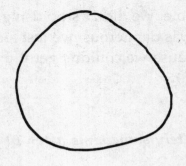

# The World (or a (or a squishy tomato)

ANYWAY, when we first got up here we did try to have a secret wigglers conversation using the glow from Grandma's teeth to illuminate our earlobes, but unfortunately everyone was so desperate to have their say that the enormous volume of flapping earlobes created such a strong wind that the roof of the neighbour's place actually began to blow off.

So then we tried an ancient American Indian device called a 'talking stick'. This means that only the person holding the stick is allowed to talk, and it's a very good way to stop everyone babbling at once. But unfortunately it was too dark to see the stick and we had to stop passing it round after four cameramen accidentally got poked in the eye and the Pip got it stuck up his nose.

(Please Note: We didn't stop using the stick because it was dangerous, we just stopped using it because we couldn't get it out of the Pip's nostril.)

## Approximately some time after 10 pm

We're still sitting on the roof trying to work out how to have a conversation but now I can hear someone who sounds exactly like Dick Witt talking through my cameraman's headphones. From the sound of his screams I think he must be panicking.

## Some time after that

The director's voice is shrill and aggressive and he's yelling 'Tell them to do something, tell them to do something!!!!'

Obviously the fact that hardly anyone is watching **Trotting with the Trotters** is a terrible situation for Dick Witt and the program makers, but personally I think it's fabulous. I mean, now that I'm over my initial embarrassment that we're not even interesting enough to seize the attention of those millions of people who tune in daily to just watch anything, even a 24-hour weather channel, I'm actually very glad that no-one's watching.

You see, I originally thought that having everyone watch would encourage me to be truly me, but now I realise that the first thing I need is to learn how to be truly me when I'm completely alone. You know, going to sleep, waking up, sitting on the toilet (assuming I ever get to go to one ever again). So now that I know that no-one is watching, I feel that this is my chance to actually really, really be me, because myself and my family have already lost the popularity contest, so what else have we got to lose? (I know you're thinking that I have my pride and my dignity and I could lose both of them but the fact of the matter is that I lost both of those years ago when I had to be hospitalised after accidentally adhering a panty pad upside down.)

But anyway,
enough of that.
The question is,
who is the real me?
Oooooooooooooooooooooooooooooooooooooooo ohhhh, exciting,

Dear Diary,

  We're still sitting on the roof but the difference now is that I've finally had the opportunity to tell everyone in the family about the postponement of tonight's elimination and the impending cancellation of the show. (Yes, I confess it was me who was grabbing for the talking stick and accidentally stuck it up the Pip's nose.) Anyway, now my entire family looks very, very sad and they seem unable to form a sentence. Of course with half my family this is completely normal, but in the case of a few this is an absolute rarity. I mean, Grandma, Babette and my mother could all talk the legs off iron pots. In fact, once my mother talked the leg off a one-legged man and he rolled all the way down the hill and ended up stuck in a drainpipe with seventeen tennis balls and a very squished hub cap.

*A bit after about ten-thirty pm*

Because I've got everyone's attention, and no-one else seems able to speak, I've decided to make the most of this opportunity to not only discuss our plight but to also grow as a human being by discussing everything I've ever wanted to talk about with my family. I've decided to start with the colour my parents originally painted my nursery.

They painted it black.

### Maybe 11 pm

Well that's rude! I'd just finished criticising my parents for the negative influences their paint choice had on me and was about to move on to the detrimental effects of being given my own shopping trolley at the age of six when I'd actually asked for a pony, and all of a sudden I heard the director say through the cameraman's headphones, 'Tell the chick with the mouth to move on or the show is going to be cancelled right now.'

What a spoilsport. Well if he doesn't like my talking then I think I might just shut up and see how he likes that. Oh yes, I think I'll shut up for ages and really make him squirm with agonised anticipation.

## Maybe one second later

Okay, enough silence, I nearly went mad!

So back to the dilemma. I guess if I can't talk about how my family has pretty well ruined my life so far I may as well talk to my family about what they want to do about the show. And I guess that means that we are going to have to openly and honestly communicate for the very first time in our lives.

I'm not sure if this conversation will be interesting enough for Dick Witt's high standards so while the rest of us talk I've asked Miss Priss and Bum Face to do a bit of a tap dance on a corner of the roof.

## 11 pm and forty-three seconds

Oh, they both just said they can't because there isn't a tap up here.

## 11 pm and round about a minute

Okay, I've now asked my family if they want
to keep on with the show until 9 am
tomorrow morning or if they want to quit
now, and they all said they want to keep on
until tomorrow because they want to be in the
running for the money and they are also
hoping a hot breakfast will be provided. So I
guess the issue here is what can we do to be
more interesting to make sure that Dick Witt
keeps the show on the air? I guess basically
we've got to think about what people love to
watch on TV:
   sport
   gardening
   cooking
   home renovations
   quiz shows
   blondes
   and bosoms.

Wow, not looking good for my family so far.

***11 pm and two minutes***
***Still on the roof getting blown about***

Dear Diary,

We're all still sitting on the roof, occasionally hanging on for dear life when a bit of a breeze picks up, but basically just wondering how to make ourselves more interesting. Babette suggested we dye our hair blonde, get breast implants and start to play football or cricket, but Grandma says that she's pretty well done all that and no-one ever said it made her more interesting. And then the Pip agreed, because apparently he's tried it too (yep, including the implants).

My father suggested that he himself might be more interesting if he learnt to speak Spanish or Greek. Miss Priss thought that she might be more interesting if she got a boyfriend who worked in a circus. Bum Face said that she could be more interesting if she drew a bum on the back of her head as well as having one on the front, and my mother said she could make herself more interesting by using cornflour instead of plain flour in all her baking recipes.

I'm thinking that maybe we should give up.
And I'm thinking it out loud.

## 11 pm and three minutes

Dear Diary,

Everyone is trying to convince me that we can be interesting and popular if we really try, but I know we can't. My family and I are hopeless and I realise this as I stare at them all huddled on the roof in the special 'roof picnic' outfits my mother rapidly made for us using sleeping bags and hats made out of oven mitts.

Let's be honest here, my family is never, ever, ever going to be intergalactically popular because they don't fit the image. We're not rich, or beautiful. We're not *Days of Our Lives*. We're an ad for a cheap car stereo that comes with a free foot spa.

If we really want to hold the world's attention then we have no choice but to marry Brad Pitt, or design a new diet, or have an affair with Liz Hurley, or get pregnant to a millionaire, or have really famous parents, or really long legs, or a drug addiction, or threaten to blow up the world, or rob a bank, or start a cult in Wilgoolga! And even then the show would still need car chases and police interrogations and home renovations and scandalous revelations. And you know what I reckon? I reckon that just ain't us.

And you know what else I reckon? I reckon that a squashed loaf of bread doesn't taste as nice, and that no matter what anyone says you can wear red and green together. AND finally I reckon that the only way any member of our family can make themselves more interesting for the viewers is by being someone else. And what is the point in that!

I guess Dwayne, my ex-boyfriend, will think I'm a failure for what I'm about to do ... but then again, he did tell me to take a good long look at myself. And besides, the only person who needs to think of me as a winner or loser is me. And I think that standing up for yourself makes you a winner. So I'm going to tell Dick Witt that I quit.

### 11 pm and four minutes

Oh, Dick Witt just said that I don't need to tell him because he's already heard everything because I was thinking out loud.

Okay, well I guess that's that then and now I'll climb off the roof and leave my family to continue to try and justify their own existence while telling 'why did the chicken cross the road?' jokes.

P.S. to get to the other slide


***11 pm and four minutes and eleven seconds***
***Climbing off the roof***

Dear Diary,
   Well, now I'm climbing down off the roof and back through the skylight in the kitchen ceiling. I'm possibly making myself sound more glamorous than I really am by saying that I'm 'climbing' off the roof, because it's a bit hard to move when you're dressed in a sleeping bag and I'm really just sliding out of control on my bum. I guess it's lucky I'm wearing an oven mitt on my head that can double as a crash-helmet.

## 11.05 pm and a bruised bottom

Anyway, I'm all alone now in the kitchen except for my cameraman who says he's going to keep filming me for the next hour no matter how interesting or dull I am. When he first told me this I thought it was because he wanted to make sure I was all right and to console me in case I was distressed, but he's since told me that it's because he really wants to be able to invoice for another full hour up until midnight, rather than just five minutes past eleven.

## 11 pm and six minutes

I think I'll go for a walk. (That'll test the length of the cameraman's extension cord.) Yep, now that I'm no longer planning on playing the game I'm free to come and go as I choose. So I think I'll just slip into something a little less uncomfortable than a sleeping bag and oven mitt, open the front door, step out into the world that finds me dull and not worth knowing, and go walk around this suburb in my apparently uninteresting, uncharismatic, uninspiring way.

**11 pm and six and a bit minutes**

Well here we go. As soon as I step through the door, cross the lawn and go out through the front gate I am officially out of the game.

Okay then ...

I'm opening the door.

Oh my gosh.

OH MY GOSH!

# OH MY GOSH!!!!

Gasp,

*11 pm and six and a half minutes*
*At the front door*

Dear Diary,
   There is a whole stack of people standing on our front lawn and they're all yelling,

# 'Go back in the house, Fleur. Don't step outside!'

   I guess they must think I'm so tragic that I shouldn't be allowed out in public. But what are they doing here? How did they know I was coming out the door? How do most of them know who I am?

*11 pm and six and three-quarter minutes*

Dear Diary,
   I can hear Dick Witt speaking through my cameraman's headphones. He's saying the ratings are suddenly sky-rocketing because

with all my talk of individuality, failure and success 'we've hit the human chord'.

# What? And what chord were we hitting before the foodless picnic — the orang-utan at the zoo chord, or the algae at the bottom of a fish pond chord?

Well that's all fine and fabulous that we've hit 'the human chord', but I'm still walking out that door, even if it's to be confronted by my enemies. Damn it, I have no choice. This loser needs some time to walk and think and no-one is going to stop me!!!!!!

**11 pm and seven minutes**

Dear Diary,
   Okay, I just stepped onto the lawn and the crowd picked me up and threw me back inside the house.
   Why, I ask you. Why?
   I mean, they've coped with having me in the neighbourhood all my life so I don't really see

why I should be banished now. Yes, no, I shouldn't be, that's right!

Sure I peed on the garden and a bit went down the neighbours' driveway but other than that I haven't been that revolting! In fact, I actually think that I'm quite considerate. I don't steal neighbours' flowers from their gardens or ride my bike into people's parked cars or play music really loudly or put firecrackers in strangers' letterboxes. I mean, Grandma may do all those things but I don't. So why should I be sent back into the house?

# Damn it, I refuse to be!

I'm going to take a deep breath and run as fast as I can all the way through that crowd.

Long live me,

## 11 pm and seven and a half minutes

Okay, they threw me back in the house again.

## 11.07 pm and forty-two seconds

Dear Diary,
   As soon as I recover I'm going to try getting
out of here once more, but this time I'm going
to jump into the air and walk over the top of
the crowd's heads so that it's harder for
everyone's arms to reach out and grab me.


   Okay, won't be long now, just a moment
while I recover.



   Okay, a moment more.



   Yes, still recovering.

Perhaps you might like to take a break at this point, dear Diary, and go out and get a glass of milk and a biscuit because I'm just feeling a bit of pressure to recover here and I don't think the pressure is really helping.

Okay, I've recovered now and am about to jump into the air and walk, no run, over everyone's heads.

Wish me luck,

**11.07 pm and three-quarters of a minute**

Dear Diary,

Sorry, I'm going to have to leave another big space here because it seems like I did jump in the air but unfortunately missed everyone's heads and just landed crash-bang on the ground and knocked myself out on the decoration Mum made for the middle of the lawn using an old toilet seat and a pile of bricks to symbolise the circle of life.

Ouch,

*fleur*

### 11.15 pm

Dear Diary,

There's a whole bunch of people standing around. Gee, I hope they don't kick and punch me.

### 11.15 and a quarter pm

Okay. I feel a bit better now. I'm ready to escape. Up I get, ready, set, go!

# QUICK!

# BACK TO

# THE HOUSE!

**11.17 pm**

Okay, I'm back in the house and now I can hear everyone chanting

## 'Fleur!
## Fleur!
## Fleur!
## Fleur!'

I'm a little scared and I want to go home. To Alice in Wonderland's house.

**11.17 pm and a quarter of a minute**

Oh no! Now to top it all off the floor manager has come clip-clopping in her enormous high heels, carrying a note that says, 'If you don't rejoin the show then no-one will win the money.'

What a disaster. Now I have to decide whether to betray myself and go back to the game or leave the game and betray my family by forcing them to forfeit a million dollars.

Maybe I really do need a body double after all,

***11.18 and a half pm***
***Near the front door***

Okay, I need to speak to someone who will
tell me what's going on. I need someone who's
wise and honest and insightful. I think I need
Oprah or someone from *Playschool* or maybe
even Santa.
Love,
Sad and confused,

***11.19 pm***

Dear Diary,
The floor manager just handed me a
note that said Lurline's on the phone.
Dick Witt has written in the note that even
though I'm not supposed to have outside
contact with anyone he will bend a rule and
let me talk to her because he thinks she
might give me sensible advice. Fat chance of
that. Lurline hasn't done anything sensible
since 1993.

But I do need someone to talk to so even though Lurline isn't wise, honest or insightful, I guess she'll have to do.

## February 4th

*12.32 am*

Dear Diary,

Well I've just got off the phone to Lurline who it seems now suddenly wants to be my best friend! I haven't got a clue what she was rabbiting on about but she sure rabbited on about it. She went on and on and on and on and as I listened to her voice rattle on like a cicada on a hot summer's day it sort of made me really stressed.

In fact it's made me so stressed I can't seem to focus on any thought and my eyes are rolling round in my head and I'm getting a massive headache. We don't have any headache pills here — well not any that Mum hasn't knitted, so I think I'd better go to Babette's bedroom to find the potion she always sips to make her as calm as a 'goddess'. (It doesn't seem to work very well on her, but let's face it, it's the only option I've got.)

**12.34 am**
**In the cupboard**

Okay, I'm in Babette's cupboard now and I've found a whole lot of bottles. They look like those little whisky bottles that you get on planes but the labels have been removed so I guess Babette must just be recycling the bottles and putting her homemade potions inside.

Ooops, someone's coming. I'm going to grab a bottle, drink it and then go down and make a calm and rational decision.

**12.35 am**

Okay soi drankthe potion and I shouldn't have. Don'tyouever doit anadnow I'm backdosntaurs. I think I musthav rolled.

I cant walk atthamoment because I'm sorelaxed buthtegood thingis my stresshas gone and now I can think reallyreallyreally reallyreallyreallyreallyreallyreally clearly. So I'll have a a reallreallyreallyreallyreallyreally reallyreally god think about whattooo doooo as soon asi've had a tiny weeny weenyweeny sleep burp. ZZZZZZZZZZZ ZZZZZZZZZZ ZZZZ ZZZZZZZZZZZZZZZZZZ ZZZZZZZZZZZZZZZZZZ ZZZZZZZZZZZZZZZZZZZZZZZZZZZZZZZZZZZZZZZZZZZ ZZZZZZZZZZZZZZZZZZZZZZZZZZZZZZZZZZZZZZZZZZZ ZZZZZZZZZZZZZZZZZZZZZZZZZZZZZZZZZZZZZZZZZZZ ZZZZZZZZZZZZZZZZZZZZZZZZZZZZZZZZZZZZZZZZZZZ ZZZZZZZZZZZZZZZZZZZZZZZZZZZZZZZZZZZZZZZZZZZ ZZZZZZZZZZZZZZZZZZZZZZZZZZZZZZZZZZZZZZZZZZZ ZZZZZZZZZZZZZZZZZZZZZZZZZZZZZZZZZZZZZZZZZZZ ZZZZZZZZZZZZZZZZZZZZZZZZZZZZZZZZZZZZZZZZZZZ ZZZZZZZZZZZZZZZZZZZZZZZZZZZZZZZZZZZZZZZZZZZ ZZZZZZZZZZZZZZZZZZZZZZZZZZZZZZZZZZZZZZZZZZZ ZZZZZZZZZZZZZZZZZZZZZZZZZZZZZZZZZZZZZZZZZZZ ZZZZZZZZZZZZZZZZZZZZZZZZZZZZZZZZZZZZZZZZZZZ ZZZZZZZZZZZZZZZZZZZZZZZZZZZZZZZZZZZZZZZZZZZ ZZZZZZZZZZZZZZZZZZZZZZZZZZZZZZZZZZZZZZZZZZZ ZZZZZZZZZZZZZZZZZZZZZZZZZZZZZZZZZZZZZZZZZZZ ZZZZZZZZZZZZZZZZZZZZZZZZZZZZZZZZZZZZZZZZZZZ ZZZZZZZZZZZZZZZZZZZZZZZZZZZZZZZZZZZZZZZZZZZ ZZZZZZZZZZZZZZZZZZZZZZZZZZZZZZZZZZZZZZZZZZZ ZZZZZZZZZZZZZZZZZZZZZZZZZZZZZZZZZZZZZZZZZZZ

ZZZZZZZZZZZZZZZZZZZZZZZZZZZZZZZZZZZZZZZZZZZZ
ZZZZZZZZZZZZZZZZZZZZZZZZZZZZZZZZZZZZZZZZZZZZZ
ZZZZZZZZZZZZZZZZZZZZZZZZZZZZZZZZZZZZZZZZZZZZZ
ZZZZZZZZZZZZZZZZZZZZZZZZZZZZZZZZZZZZZZZZZZZZZ
ZZZZZZZZZZZZZZZZZZZZZZZZZZZZZZZZZZZZZZZZZZZZZ
ZZZZZZZZZZZZZZZZZZZZZZZZZZZZZZZZZZZZZZZZZZZZZ
ZZZZZZZZZZZZZZZZZZZZZZZZZZZZZZZZZZZZZZZZZZZZZ
ZZZZZZZZZZZZZZZZZZZZZZZZZZZZZZZZZZZZZZZZZZZZZ
ZZZZZZZZZZZZZZZZZZZZZZZZZZZZZZZZZZZZZZZZZZZZZ
ZZZZZZZZZZZZZZZZZZZZZZZZZZZZZZZZZZZZZZZZZZZZZ
ZZZZZZZZZZZZZZZZZZZZZZZZZZZZZZZZZZZZZZZZZZZZZ.
ZZZZZZZZZZZZZZZZZZZZZZZZZZZZZZZZZZZZZZZZZZZZZ
ZZZZZZZZZZZZZZZZZZZZZZZZZZZZZZZZZZZZZZZZZZZZZ
ZZZZZZZZZZZZZZZZZZZZZZZZZZZZZZZZZZZZZZZZZZZZZ
ZZZZZZZZZZZZZZZZZZZZZZZZZZZZZZZZZZZZZZZZZZZZZ
ZZZZZZZZZZZZZZZZZZZZZZZZZZZZZZZZZZZZZZZZZZZZZ
ZZZZZZZZZZZZZZZZZZZZZZZZZZZZZZZZZZZZZZZZZZZZZ
ZZZZZZZZZZZZZZZZZZZZZZZZZZZZZZZZZZZZZZZZZZZZZ
ZZZZZZZZZZZZZZZZZZZZZZZZZZZZZZZZZZZZZZZZZZZZZ
ZZZZZZZZZZZZZZZZZZZZZZZZZZZZZZZZZZZZZZZZZZZZZ
ZZZZZZZZZZZZZZZZZZZZZZZZZZZZZZZZZZZZZZZZZZZZZ
ZZZZZZZZZZZZZZZZZZZZZZZZZZZZZZZZZZZZZZZZZZZZZ
ZZZZZZZZZZZZZZZZZZZZZZZZZZZZZZZZZZZZZZZZZZZZZ
ZZZZZZZZZZZZZZZZZZZZZZZZZZZZZZZZZZZZZZZZZZZZZ
ZZZZZZZZZZZZZZZZZZZZZZZZZZZZZZZZZZZZZZZZZZZZZ
ZZZZZZZZZZZZZZZZZZZZZZZZZZZZZZZZZZZZZZZZZZZZZ
ZZZZZZZZZZZZZZZZZZZZZZZZZZZZZZZZZZZZZZZZZZZZZ
ZZZZZZZZZZZZZZZZZZZZZZZZZZZZZZZZZZZZZZZZZZZZZ.

## 4 am. Yes that's right, four am in the morning!

Dear Diary,

Oh my headache has got worse! The crowd is still chanting outside my window but it seems that I managed to fall asleep there for a few hours. I've actually just been woken by a figure that looks like the ghost of Dame Edna, but I suspect might be the floor manager.

She's coming toward me with yet another note. My gosh! This is worse than junk email.

Anyway the note says she's waking me to tell me that she'll be waking me in four hours.

Fabulous, now turn the light back out, clip clop from the room, and

let

me

get

some

sleep.

Z  Z  z  z  z  z  z .

## It's 8 am

Dear Diary,

The floor manager has just woken me.

Apparently in one hour the nation, the

world, or maybe just one person (i.e. the host), will be voting for the winner of one million dollars.

I can tell from the shouting and chanting in the garden that it won't be me. They're all relentlessly yelling my name like they want to hang me. But I guess the fact that I'm still here means that the game can continue and that at least someone in my family will be the winner of a million dollars. So maybe someone somewhere in the universe will like me for that. You know what I mean — maybe someone somewhere in the universe will like me for helping to make someone else shine like a star.

Yeah, maybe someone will. But I doubt it.

I guess it would be fair if Mum won because she's pretty well invested her life in all of us. But then again so has Dad, so maybe he should get it too. But then the problem is that they've both remarried losers and if either Mum or Dad were to win then they will obviously share the money with their new partners and that would make Mum and Dad the losers. Miss Priss would keep all the money to herself, which of course is better than giving it to losers, but then is also very selfish. Bum Face would probably share it with her cockroach boyfriend and then he'd probably dump her for a rat or a nit or a maggot or something and run off with the money to Rio.

Maybe Grandma should win. But Grandma's never done anything for anyone in her entire life. Actually, that's not true. She's done an awful lot for an awful lot of blokes (but I don't think their wives are very pleased about it). And I guess that's actually a very good point, because the winner of the money will not necessarily be the person who I think is the most deserving, it will be the one who the audience likes most.

Which actually makes it all even weirder because it's not like anyone in my family has actually done anything to make themselves likeable. I mean, sure, Mum whipped up a dinner last night using nothing but birdseed and two old pillows, and after dinner the Pip did the cancan while singing *Advance Australia Fair*. But I wonder what people are going to judge us by. The colour of our hair, our height, the shape of our teeth, the tone of our skin, the fact that Babette sings German opera in her sleep?

Confused and alone,

*8.27 am*

Dear Diary,

Oh no, this is going from bad to worse to unbelievably bad to even worse. Apparently they're going to vote for us according to whether or not they like the 'vote for me' speeches we're all supposed to give, one after the other, starting in about three minutes.

Oh fabulous again. Not.

*8.30 am*
*In the living room*

Dear Diary,

We're in the living room now. The whole family has been reunited and we're just about to start the speeches but we have to wait until Dick Witt stops screaming into the cameramen's headphones. Interestingly, for once he's not screaming with anguish or anger but apparently with delight. He's just heard that the ratings went through the roof overnight. So Dick is screaming with joy.

*8.34 am*

We're all sitting on the knitted furniture waiting for our speeches to start. But first the host has decided that he needs to reappear on camera and make a speech about himself. Funny how he can be centre stage, have all the attention, talk and talk and talk and never actually answer the question on everyone's lips. i.e. why he's wearing a dead rat as a ponytail.

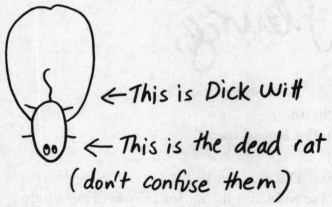

←This is Dick Witt

← This is the dead rat (don't confuse them)

*8.49 am*

Dear Diary,
Well the good thing about Dick Witt giving a speech is that it's used up a lot of time that we would otherwise have had to fill with our speeches so now we only have a minute each to try to impress the audience.

Babette has just started and appears to be stealing heavily from a combination of the speeches of Martin Luther King and slogans from Coke commercials. She's standing on a chair presumably because she thinks the extra height will give her power, but because the cameraman can't make his camera go any higher he's actually only filming her knees.

Babette should have painted faces on them.

### 8.52 am

Miss Priss is up now. Apparently she'd prepared a speech about the bravery of the individual, but unfortunately she felt too scared to actually deliver it by herself. So instead she's performing a scene from Harry Potter with Bum Face. (I don't mean like the title of the movie is *Harry Potter with Bum Face*. What I mean is that Miss Priss is performing with Bum Face.) It's the scene where Harry flies for the first time so Bum Face is pretending to be the broom and Miss Priss is sitting on her while saying 'Whoosh, woooosh.'

I wonder if anyone watching these two will vote for them to win the million dollars. I suppose someone might. I mean, people drive cars with their school sticker on the rear window so I guess humans will basically do anything.

### 8.54 am

Okay, the Pip is up next and he's decided that the best way to show that he should win the million dollars is to just hold a copy of his bank statement up to the camera and then quietly sob. I guess he's trying to show how financially poor he is, but all he's proving is that he has no pride and no dignity and is therefore emotionally poverty struck as well.

But you know what? I bet someone somewhere votes for this fat bald boiled-egg-looking guy to win the money.

Probably someone who really likes Humpty Dumpty.

### 8.55 am

I just realised that I forgot to tell you, dear Diary, that Dick Witt apparently worked out who should go first, second and third et cetera by pulling our names out of something (presumably a hat and not his bum). I know already that I'm last, Dad is before me, Mum is after him and then Grandma is on after Mum. That's if Grandma makes it that far. From where I'm sitting she's flashing on and off. This is a warning that she's about to go red, or else firm evidence that she's purposely stolen and swallowed the light from the top of a police car. If she starts to make a siren noise, I'll know she's faking the near death thing.

I waved at Grandma a moment ago to see if she wanted any help, and she smiled and nodded in that special way she does when she pretends that she's a nice sweet old lady and then mouthed the words, 'You try and stop me winning this million bucks and I'll drag you through the cobbled streets tied to the back of a wagon.'

(Obviously Grandma has forgotten that cars have been invented.)

Anyway, as I said, it's Dad's turn now and he's decided to read a short speech that Babette wrote for him about how deserving he is to win the money. It would appear that the main reason he's deserving is because he had the wisdom to marry Babette, but other reasons he has recited include:

1/ the goodness and love he brings to the world

2/ the family he supports (this is mentioned

in a 'oh poor him, look at his pathetic family' way, and

3/ the fact that he is a brilliant inventor who designed such things as the Warm Fridge and the Inflatable Meal.

I have to confess that Dad is finding this pretty hard to say because he's really not into self-promotion. He's a shy man, a humble man, a reserved man who wears three pairs of underpants on top of each other every single day. And you know, I can tell by the way that Dad is standing that he really doesn't want to win the money anyway. His feet are turned inward, his shoulders are stooped, his fingers are crossed behind his back, he's shaking his head, and he has his back to the camera.

At this stage I'd vote for him as the winner. But wait a minute, because here comes Mum, or at least someone who used to look like Mum before they dressed up as a four year old in rags and wandered across the living room holding a sign that says 'Please help me I am an orphan'.

(I know that sounds deceptive and self-serving, and far more likely to be something that I'd do, but you know what I reckon Mum would do if she won the million dollars? Give away every cent of it.)

## 8.57 am

It's Grandma's turn now. She's been announced but hasn't walked into the centre of the room. Instead she's sitting in her chair gasping for air and mumbling something like, 'Don't bother about me I'm just a poor old woman who's lived through countless wars, depressions, recessions and embarrassing fashion fads and who is possibly going to live for a very, very long time with hardly a penny to my name for my entire life I've done everything I could for others but I am so selfless I can't actually mention the things that I've done I'm also so selfless that I couldn't possibly ask you to throw a penny my way because there are others who are more needy than me but may I point out however that none of those more needy people is actually in the same room as me competing for the money.'

Oh my goodness. The cameramen are crying. Well if they're any indication of the way the world is going to fall for Grandma then I almost couldn't be bothered getting up and having my turn at speaking. I mean, if they're willing to choose a woman who claims she can hardly breathe and then in one enormous breath delivers a sentence that not only contains 146 words but would require the lung

273

capacity of a deep-sea pearl diver then I really couldn't be bothered trying because I can't compete with that.

I mean, let's be honest. I can't compete with any of them.

Oh my goodness, it's my turn.

**8.58 am**
*Centre stage*

Dear Diary,

I'm standing centre stage, i.e. just next to the banana lounge in the middle of the living room, but I don't know how I got here. I haven't a clue what I should do now and I feel like I need a bit of grounding so that's why I'm just sort of standing here continuing to write in my diary.

I really don't know what to do. Should I speak, should I dance, should I pretend to juggle, should I tell that joke about the ... oh no, I can't remember the joke. I feel so exposed, so vulnerable and naked. Do I have any clothes on? I'd better check. Yes I do. Well that's good.

It's a pity I don't remember the joke because it would have been perfect. It might not have won me a million dollars but it would definitely have given my mouth something to do other than hang open like an electrocuted fish.

I can hear the clock ticking. That's my time tick-ticking away. That's my pride tick-ticking away. But I can't think, I can't move. All of me, my mind, my heart and my body is frozen. I feel like one of Bum Face's pieces of used chewing gum which she puts in her shoe overnight so she can chew it again in the morning (the gum, not the shoe).

Everyone in the world must be cringing with embarrassment while they sit and watch me. Everyone must be so humiliated for me, so ashamed on my behalf.

Everyone must be wishing that I never existed.

### 8.59 am

I just heard someone in here whisper, 'Come on Fleur, you can do it.' It's Miss Piggy, the floor manager, and her voice is surprisingly deep. So she can speak after all. Well isn't that weird, because other than Dwayne I don't know anyone who's that kind and supportive — well except for the school counsellor who said wonderful things about me at the school dance, and then fell flat on her face dead drunk.

## 8.59 and a bit am

Hey wait a minute, a few more people outside just said it. 'Come on, Fleur, you can do it.'

## 8.59 and two bits am

Hey hold on now, a whole crowd is roaring,
# 'Come on Fleur you can do it.'

And you know what?

I can.

## 8.59 and a half am

Dear Diary,

I've started my speech and I'm not even shaking. I'm just smiling at the camera and telling the truth. I can't compete for this money. I am not nicer or kinder or better than anyone else in my family. (Well, I am nicer and kinder and better than a few people in my family but I'm certainly not going to mention names.) And anyway, the point is, I'm just me. I can't juggle or belly dance or recite poetry, in fact I can barely make a cup of tea. But the one thing I can do and plan to get better at is simply being me.

I don't need this money. I know the million dollars won't make me happy and I know it won't bring me love. I know that true happiness comes from the heart, not from possessions that money can buy.

I think I've learnt a lot so far, even just in the last twenty-four hours, and I have to say thank you to all the people outside for their support and the various members of my family who probably didn't even know that they were encouraging me to be me. So I'm praising my family members and trying to think of special things to say about each and every one of them ... but unfortunately I can't think of anything so I'm just bouncing over that subject.

### 8.59 am and half a bit

I can see the host reach for the gong that will
say that my time is up and all of a sudden I
know the absolute truth of what I want to say.
Don't give me the money, give it to someone
else. I have my family and I have my friends,
even if they are occasionally two-faced and
unsupportive. I have my heart, my mind and
my health, and I'm rich enough as it is.

### 8.59 am and fifty-nine seconds

I think my own speech just made me feel sick.

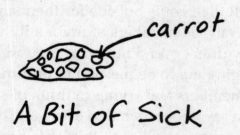

carrot

A Bit of Sick

**9 am**

Dear Diary,
  The gong just went and I'm walking back to the knitted couch to sit with my family like a row of lemmings waiting for a bus. Except we're not waiting for a bus at all, we're waiting for the world votes to be tallied and the announcement of the winner.

**9 am and five seconds.**

Still waiting.

**9 am and thirteen seconds**

The host has just announced that the creator of the show will be announcing the winner. Wow, this show has a creator! How fabulous, how powerful, how incredibly god-like!
I wonder if he'll be wearing a white kaftan and a golden beard.

**9 am and forty-five seconds**

Oh my goodness, it's Miss Piggy, the floor manager.

### 9 am and fifty seconds

Oh my God, she's taking off her dress ... and her hair ... oh, thank goodness, it's a wig. And what about the hairs all over the legs ... oh, they're hers ... I mean his!

### 9 am and fifty-five seconds

Oh my God, it's Dwayne!

### 9 am and fifty-nine seconds

He's ignoring me and standing in the middle of the living room right next to the knitted banana chair, preparing to announce the winner.

And outside I can hear the crowd loudly chanting my name.

Fleur

Fleur

Fleur

Fleur

Fleur

Fleur

Fleur

Fleur

Fleur

Fleur

Fleur

Fleur

Fleur

Fleur

Fleur

### 9 am and one minute

Dwayne just said that the winner is Grandma.

### 9 am and one minute and 22 seconds

I knew that Dick Witt was manipulating the votes. Wow, Grandma must be one hell of a kisser.

### 9 am and one and a half minutes

Grandma just squeaked and jumped out of her chair and fell in a heap on the floor.

### 9 am and two minutes

Dear Diary,
  Grandma's dead. I can tell because she's gone purple and that's the colour we always go in my family when we have kicked the bucket so hard we've even gone past red.
  Oops,

# A Red Head (Grandma)

## The rest of February

I'm pretty sad.

# March 4th

Dear Diary,

Well it's a month later and Grandma isn't on the living room floor anymore, she's in a vase on the mantelpiece instead.

And you know what? I'm happy that the million dollars that Grandma won was left to all of us in her will. So now we actually buy clothes instead of making them out of cupcake papers and we live in a mansion and we help the poor and the needy and I hang out with my family and we laugh and hug all the time. Babette and Dad split up and the Pip and my mum split up and now I'm so cool with my family that I even invite them along to parties and dances just so we can spend more time together. Miss Priss has become a supermodel, and every now and then I go out with Dwayne ... and Bum Face, who happens to be Dwayne's new girlfriend.

Bum Face (in disguise
as a normal person)

*Two minutes later*

Only joking!!!!!
   Grandma's last will was written in 1933
and in it she left all her wealth to some guy
with a cute butt she met on a train near
Hotbot so my family will never see a cent of
the million bucks. I still live with my family in
the house that my father extended fifteen

years ago using bricks that my mother knitted.
Babette is still with my father and still looks
like she has a possum on her head. And the
Pip is still with my mother and still looks like
Mr Potato Head without the charisma. Miss
Priss has not become a supermodel, she's
become a library monitor at school instead,
and we don't help the poor or the needy and
we don't all party together, although
occasionally I do go out with Dwayne ... and
Bum Face, who happens to be his new
girlfriend. (That bit was true.)

Dwayne has also moved back into our house.
Turns out that when he moved out he didn't
go far ... because he was sleeping under the
shrub in the front garden that Dad had pruned
in the shape of a shrub. So yes, they were his
pillow and sleeping bag that I found when I
was peeing all that time ago.

So everything is pretty much the same as
it ever was ... except for the fact that the
pimple on my forehead finally disappeared
and now I've had my birthday. So I'd better
hurry up and write my first hit song which
I think I'll either call *Oh My Goodness I'm
so Mature and Fabulous* or *I Used to Think
That Life Sucked, But That's When I was
a Sucker.*

### Thirty seconds after the two minutes later

So basically that's it. I've grown wiser and very, very kind and loving. Everyone just thinks it's a stage I'm going through, like the time I dyed my fingernails purple with beetroot juice because I wasn't allowed to buy real nailpolish, but I think I might stay like this forever (wiser and kinder, not purple fingernailed).

So goodbye, dear Diary, good luck, bon voyage, you've been a good friend and a good confidante and much better than Lurline because I know you won't tell anybody.

Love,

P.S. This next bit is for my family just in case they happen to ever read this diary. Firstly, anything you think is bad about you in here is just an absolutely hilarious joke you didn't understand. Mum and Dad, I love you. Miss Priss, I'm sure that one day you will be a fabulous supermodel, if someone stretches you and transplants your head. And Bum Face, I'm sorry for calling you Bum Face for your whole life because your face doesn't look so much like a bum anymore. It kind of looks more like two bosoms.

P.P.S. None of you should be reading my private diary anyway.

P.P.P.S. Dwayne and Bum Face aren't really an item. Nup! Dwayne and I are. I think I love him and have said that if he practises his tongue kissing I'll kiss him in a month, so he's outside groping a mango.

P.P.P.P.S. Looks like I will be writing another diary after all.

## THE END

# Other books by
# Gretel Killeen . . .

My life is a toilet

me

GRETEL KILLEEN

# My life is a wedgie

## GRETEL KILLEEN

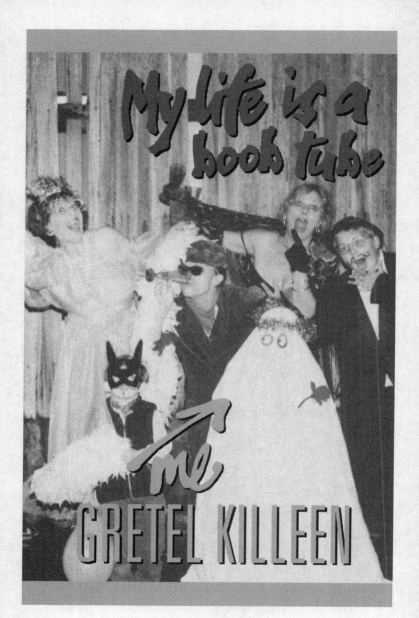

# My life is a boob tube

## Me

### GRETEL KILLEEN

**S**ome days are sunny,
some days it pours.
Some shoes fit,
some make your feet sore.
Some TV is funny,
some TV's a bore.
And most mothers are perfect,
but every now and then
one comes along who is very,
very,
very,
naughty.
Zed and Pink are a normal brother and
sister except for one extremely strange
thing ... their mum is a very naughty mother.
Fall in love with the first of this fabulously
funny series about the mother who lives her
life like a kid, and the two kids who have
to raise her.

**S**ome mothers are smart,
some mothers are sweet.

Some mothers are cuddly,
some mothers are neat.

Some mothers are perfect in every way. But one
mother is, well, what can I say?

One mother is ...very, very,
very, very naughty.

Welcome (with a big wink) to the second book in this
hilarious series about a mother who lives her life as a
kid, and her two kids who have to raise her.

Enjoy the drama, delight and
absolutely breathtaking bizarreness of
the Very Naughty Mother's naughty runaway journey
and the extraordinary things that occur on the way.

**S**ome mothers are strict,
some mothers are whiny.

Some mothers can cook,
some mothers are tidy.

Some mothers are perfect in all that they do,
while some mothers get stuck in trouble like
glue ...

This is the story of one of those mothers —
a mother who lives her life as a kid —
and the two kids who have to raise her.

Oh, yes, this is the tale of the day that the Very
Naughty Mother interrupts a magic Kerwuffle
spell, goes invisible, gets kidnapped, nearly
turns into a gold statue, rides on a cloud and is
rescued by her two fabulous children, Zed and
Pink (who can drive and fly and spy as well).

So you have to read this book.
**Because it's fabulous!**

MY SISTER'S A YOYO

When Eppie falls into a pot hole and gets squashed to
the size of a strawberry, her brother Zeke decides to
have some fun with his yoyo.

What follows is a hilarious high tale of escape, theft,
bullies, brats, dobbers, goody-goodies, garbage trucks,
magic lamps, scabs, snot, bribery, bravery, a blind
mum, a fat nurse, a skinny teacher and a boy on a
bicycle covered in vomit – and that's only the
beginning!

## MY SISTER'S A NIGHTMARE

When tiny Eppie and Zeke finally manage to escape from a book, they accidentally end up in a rattling carriage that is part of their mother's train of thought. Unable to get off at Real World, Dream World or even Fantasy World, Zeke and Eppie find themselves hurtling toward their mother's ridiculous nightmare. What follows is a laugh-till-you-split-your-sides adventure full of googly ghosts, drastic draculas, spiralling spiders, haunted houses, vampish vampires, potent potions, rapping bats and disgusting meals that never end. Will Zeke and Eppie escape from the nightmare or will they be stuck in their mother's bad thoughts forever (along with the boyfriend she had when she was nine and a packet of chocolate biscuits)?

Gretel Killeen is the author of a million books including the hugely popular *My Life is a Toilet, My Life is a Wedgie* and *My Life is a Boob Tube.* She is published in Australia, Britain, Europe, Asia and Canada. Many of her books are best-sellers and two are sort of flops. Having started her career as a stand-up comic, Gretel appears regularly as a 'funny person' on national television and radio, and has recently hit the heights of recognisability while hosting the enormously popular *Big Brother.* Gretel is currently raising her son and daughter and running around like a headless chook.

Other books by Gretel Killeen include the *My Sister's* series, a laugh-a-minute roller-coaster ride to hilarity! and the *Very Naughty Mother* series, about a mother who lives her life as a kid, and the two kids who have to raise her.